Hired Sword

The Prince turned to Thane of The Two Swords.

"I would like to test your much-vaunted speed," he said, smiling, "and it would afford me much pleasure to chastise you. But you are too valuable to my needs to afford me this kind of self-indulgence. I will give you—one million pieces of gold if you will enter my service for three days."

Thane blinked incredulously. That kind of wealth could set up a wandering spaceman for the rest of his life!

"How about—*two* million?" he countered.

TOWER AT THE EDGE OF TIME

Lin Carter

A TOWER BOOK

TOWER AT THE EDGE OF TIME

This one is dedicated to
George Scithers,
The Hyborian Legion,
and to all the boys at the Terminus,
Owlswick, & Ft. Mudge Electrick Street
Railway.

A TOWER BOOK

Tower Publications, Inc.
185 Madison Avenue
New York, New York 10016

Printed in U.S.A.

INTRODUCTION:

Of Thane of The Two Swords and the Time Wizards of Aea

"It is written in the Eternal Scripture that one should come to whom the Tower would yield her secret. For untold billions of years hath the Tower guarded her Mystery, aye, since that the Children of Aea set forth from this Galaxy and returned to that place from whence they came in the Beginning, even to that strange region called The Fire Mist which lieth beyond the Universe of Stars.

"Throughout the six thousand years the mighty Carina Empire ruled the star worlds, the Time Priests waited and watched for his coming, and worshiped the Children of the Fire Mist, but lo! the man came not, and still the Tower stood and held her Mystery.

"And the Empire fell before the Star Rovers, and in the fullness of time, the Star Rovers fell before the wisdom of the White Adepts of Parlion, and lo! the man came not. And, in their despair, the Time Priests said the Scripture lied and the hero of the Quest should never come, and even that the Tower Beyond Time was but a thing of fable.

"*But there was in that ninth century of the Interregnum, ere yet the New Empire arose to take the place of the Old that was fallen, a man they were wont to call Thane of the Two Swords. A man of blood and steel was this Thane, a man of strange power strangely got, and for whom an even stranger Destiny was reserved . . .*"

—THE IRON BOOK OF AANTHOR

1 CITY OF A THOUSAND GODS

IT WAS THANE who crossed the abyss of the ages and stood on the very brink of Eternity . . . who found the secret of the Time Treasure . . . who saw, and laughed, and came back sane from that place beyond the Universe where no man had ever been before him, and where none should ever come again.

This was the ending. But the beginning was in the city of Zotheera on the planet Daikoon . . .

He came striding into many-templed Zotheera at that hour the Daikoona call The Death of Suns. As he strode through the Dragon Gate, the Three Suns were sinking one by one on the horizon in a blaze of golden flame.

Tall he was, and grim of face; naked, but for a loin cloth of scarlet silk, a leathern harness of belted straps set with square studs of bronze, and a vast blue cloak that swung from broad, bare shoulders. His hair poured over his brawny shoulders like a crimson flood. It was red: not rust or bronze or gold, but—*red* —an arterial crimson metallic in luster and startling to behold. From this you might have known him for a son of Zha the Jungle Planet, for only the Zhayana have such hair. Their world is rich in crystalloid mercuric sulphide, from which Alchemists derive cinnabar, and this substance permeates the soil, and the fruit of that soil, and forms a harmless residue in the bodies of the Zha-born, lending their hair that hue.

His body was that of a gladiator, or a god, magnificent in its manhood and virile strength, like the gold statue of Lionus the Hero which stands in Argion, the Trader's World, in far Orion. It was burnt a golden bronze, seared by the fierce lambda-radiation of Deep Space which penetrates every energy shield yet devised by man, and tanned by the mingled radiance of a hundred suns whose far-flung worlds had felt his tread. Lithe and tigerish he was, this Thane of the Two Swords, with eyes of cold metallic grey, like broken steel. Men stepped from his path, as they noted the grim set of his clean-shaven jaw, and the way his eyes prowled restless and roving, and how his great scarred hands brushed easy near his bare flanks, a split-second from the twin sword pommels. They knew by instinct this was a warrior whose hair-trigger reflexes could explode into a fury of slashing steel, and they shrunk aside to let him stride by.

Never before had Thane seen Zotheera, yet nothing he saw moved him, and though much was strange, he saw naught to fear. He had drunk the heady wine of adventure from a thousand cups on a hundred weird worlds ere now . . . as poet, gladiator, warrior with sword for hire, thief with a price on his head, corsair who had led wild hordes to ravage and loot rich planet ports, or wandering adventurer driven by strange thirsts to seek danger in all its thousand forms and faces.

Like one fleeing from some enormous and irreparable crime, or one seeking relief in far exotic places from the intolerable burden of lost, unforgotten love, he roamed and roved the great black spaces between the stars. In the whispering, wine-scented forests of Valthomé he had hunted the fearsome Man-Spiders with but a spear. Masked in a globe of crystal that he might breathe, he had dared the purple seas of Yaoth and visited the sea bottom cities builded of pink coral. He had hunted the Pharvisian snow tiger in the glacier-bound hills of that far world where men drink blood and swear by Silence. He had sought black pearls on the green-sanded beaches of Pelizon, where men have three eyes and fight with little ebony rods. He had ventured even into the Black Drift between the galactic arms, to dim Clesh, the world where witches rule, and where captive monsters of living stone hew from scented wood the idols of the Chaos Lords. Much had he seen, far had he wandered, and from all had he taken a certain something into himself. And there was about him an aura of strangeness and power, as some frightening and exotic fragrance which clung to him in his lone passage through strange worlds amid even stranger men.

The lean, swarthy men of Zotheera eyed him curiously as he strode past, his fiery thatch burning in the golden suns' setting. Oblique eyes followed him speculatively, gleaming from the shadows of hooded cloaks. Men of many worlds they knew, for Daikoon the Desert World is famous for her rubies, as for her gods. Hither come men from all the Near Stars, Spica V where men have purple skin and white eyes, many-gardened Athnolan and Delaquoth the Dream-world, peaceful Onaldus of the blue hills and yellow

skies, Scather and Mindanell and dim Valdorm, Az-
meryl and Besht and Harza of the Thousand Lakes.
But the Desert Warriors who watched him pass had
never seen another like this tall blue-cloaked swordsman, and they watched and wondered . . .

Zotheera is a city of many gods. All about Thane as
he stalked through the crowded ways rose temples
and shrines to all the thousand gods of space—Zargon
the Measurer, the Lord of Punishment and Reward,
and Thaxis of the Battles, Onolk the Spacegod, Maryash the Protector and Shalakh the Lord of Fortune.
There beyond the Athquom Square rose the dark
house of Malasquor of the Eleven Scarlet Hells, and
there beyond, its spires gilt with the suns' setting, rose
the temple of bearded Arnam and the goddess Sindhi.

But Thane of Zha had not come here to worship.

He strode through the city, his great blue cloak
belling wide from swinging shoulders. Down the
Street of the Brass Workers and the Avenue of the
Red Witch; through the Semmelak Quarter where
dusky silent men carve opals and worship cats, and
into the Street of the God makers, where yellow men
with shaven heads paused to watch him pass, ceasing
from their work of hewing idols from blocks of that
blood red alabaster the Tigermen of Bartosca mine
from the Red Hills in the Land of Fire.

They wondered who he was, and what strange
Doom drove him on, and whispers rose in his
wake . . .

On the street of the Wine Sellers he entered an inn
called The House of Thirteen Pleasures. He shouldered through the crowd into the smoky hall and took
a table at the rear. The host, a fat, plum purple Spi-

can brought him a flask of that rich ale they brew on Netharna. But Thane poured out the liquid on the sawdust-strewn floor and crushed the bronze bottle between the fingers of one hand into a rough ball of solid metal.

"I will drink the green wine of Bellerophon," he said softly, and the Spican stared with wide white eyes at the hand that had crushed a metal vase as another might crumple a sheet of parchment, and he brought quickly green wine in a pitcher of cut garnet. All the men stared at him, taking in the cold steel eyes and long golden body of this man, all gliding sinews and ropes and cables of sleek muscle woven over massive bones, and they kept clear of his table.

So Thane sprawled out and drank the icy, mint wine and watched the dancing girls. There were three of these, and they were girl-shaped, but Thane had walked a hundred worlds and knew them for Pseudowomen from Shuuth, and turned his attention from their voluptuous posturings and undulations.

Along the far wall of this Inn stretched a row of curtained booths. From one of these a strong white hand reached from behind hangings of violet cloth and a red stone on the forefinger of this hand, set in a band of curious green metal, flashed and winked as the finger pointed at Thane's back.

Thane, who saw nothing of this, drank his wine and wiped his lips with a scarf of golden silk he drew from a pocket pouch. Then he casually draped the scarf over his right hand where it lay idly on the table.

There was a man who stood along the marble-topped bar in the front of the Inn, among a crowd of spacemen from the nearby field, a man who constantly but without so-seeming watched that booth with the drawn curtain. He saw the white hand gesture, paid his tally, and detached himself from the throng. He strode to where Thane sat toying with the golden scarf and drinking his mint wine. Making as if to pass Thane's table, he stumbled—or seemed to stumble—over Thane's outstretched leg. Cursing vividly, the man stopped and spat on the floor between the Zhayan's spread feet.

"You slime-born jungle scum—pull in those feet or I'll hew them off and feed them to you—you stinking spawn of Hell's ninth scarlet pit—"

With eyes like chips of steel, Thane idly looked him up and down. The bravo had shoulders like an Ormisian wrestler, with the shaven pate and lobeless ears of a Chadorian nerve killer. And venomous little green eyes that flared in a tough, cold face whose nose had been broken and set badly and broken again until it was an ugly lump of cartilage.

But Thane said nothing. He smiled.

The room was suddenly quiet as a tomb. Men cleared away from the nearer tables. Tension gathered in the air, like the electric still before a storm.

The Chadorian pulled out an ugly Sirian hook sword and held it lightly in one massive hand corded and glassy with scar tissue. He sneered, thin lips peeling back from rotting teeth whose green color spelled an habituate of the Deathflower drug. Thane smiled, but did not move.

Puzzled that Thane did not rise, the Chadorian laughed: "Your girl's face under that pretty red hair looks familiar, golden boy! I think I knew your mother—wasn't she a temple slut at Ydorna's house in the Thieves' Quarter? Seems to me I bedded her once for a few coppers, and got the pox rot . . ."

Smiling gently, Thane reached over and slowly drew the golden scarf away from his right hand.

It held a laser pistol whose snout was like a cold blue eye staring directly at the Chadorian's belly.

Neither spoke or moved. The bravo went grey to the lips. He sagged, as if every drop of manhood was suddenly drained from him, and he was left weak as wax. There went through the room a susurration of indrawn breaths.

"I . . . look, buddy . . ." the Chadorian started to say with numb lips.

Thane fired.

A needle of electric-blue fire, intolerably brilliant, speared from the gun and struck the yard long Sirian hook sword near the hilt. Steel flushed dull red—then muddy yellow—then incandescently white. The sword bent, splattering the floor with smoking droplets of liquid fire, and the blade fell away like a white candle caught in the heart of a furnace.

The Chadorian screeched as a fiery spray of molten metal seared and blistered his hand. He shook the red hot hilt loose from his hand and it fell away, together with some bits of burned skin. He clutched, with his unharmed left hand, the wrist of his hideously burned right hand, and moaned from the unendurable pain. The metal tang of the hilt, coated only with a wrapping of leather thongs, had seared through leather and flesh, burning him to the bone. The pain was more intense than seemed possible.

Thane snapped off the droning laser beam and put the pistol down on the table. Then, with a lithe and lazy movement, he rose to his feet, unbuckling his swordbelt with a careless hand and leaving the clutter behind him on the table he stepped out before the moaning Chadorian and hit him twice in as many seconds.

The first blow went straight into the Chadorian's solar plexus—Thane's balled fist sank like a hammer blow into the very pit of the man's stomach, sinking in almost to the wrist. It was a terrible, crippling blow. The air whooshed from the Chadorian's lungs —his face purpled—and he folded at the middle.

The second blow was an uppercut. It rose from the level of Thane's knees—driven by the steely thews of his thighs, back, shoulders and superbly muscled arms, with every atom of strength at his command.

It caught the Chadorian on the point of his chin as he sagged, doubled over from the belly blow. It snapped him erect, actually lifting him a couple of inches off his feet. He went flying backward and came down, shattering a table into kindling . . . to stretch his six feet out on the sawdust-strewn floor. His jaw was broken in two places and he was missing four teeth. He lay there, unconscious, limp as a dead thing, scarlet blood dribbling from his crushed mouth filled with broken teeth.

As a couple of men hauled him off the floor and dragged the limp Chadorian from the Inn, Thane quietly took his seat, retrieving his swordbelt and slipping the deadly little laser pistol back in his pouch. He poured out another cup of chilled mint wine from the garnet flacon.

"Would you like to earn a hundred thousand pieces of gold?" asked a small, shriveled, sly-eyed man with butter yellow skin who slipped into a chair facing him.

2 SEVEN GOLD DRAGONS

THANE LOOKED AT HIM: Small, dwarfed, his buttery flesh tight-stretched over a bald skull, shrunken and withered with ten thousand little wrinkles, and slitted eyes of the color of black emeralds. There was about the little man something reptilian and repellant.

"Tell your Master in the third booth from the left," he said in a calm, level voice, "that I am neither to be intimidated by brute force nor bought by gold. And go away—you smell of Yoth Zembis and I dislike sorcerors."

That jarred the sly-eyed little enchanter like a slap in the teeth. His dull mineral eyes went blank for a moment as he sought for a reply.

The only thing he could think of was: "Two hundred thousand pieces—?"

Thane grinned. It was not a smile of humor, but a wolfish baring of white teeth.

"Not for two hundred million," he said. "I am *not for sale*, although I doubt your Master will believe it. From the looks of you and the flat-nosed Chadorian bully boy who is also on his payroll, I doubt your

Master has ever met anything but prostitutes. Now get away from me: I step on snakes."

The slitted eyes flashed with venomous fires.

"You must learn to address your betters in more gentle terms," the dwarfed enchanter hissed. "And I am not impressed by mere muscle any more than are you. Ere you could touch me, I could slay you where you sit in any one of thirty ways—all unpleasant."

Thane laughed.

"Oh, I doubt not you have your fangs! But there are more ways than 'mere muscle' to crush a snake—and *I* am not impressed by a dried-up renegade from the Third Circle of Goetia who has broken his vows and fled from the vengeance of his own Priesthood!"

That staggered the venomous old enchanter! He gasped at the ease with which this strange man read him.

"You—"

Thane, who took delight in acting contrary to the expectations of others, and who had long ago determined to go his own way despite whatever forms of coercion or threat or bribery were used to divert him, continued in a quiet, mocking tone of voice whose every single word was calculated to shatter the impassive Buddhalike mask of calm indifference that faced him across the table.

"Tell me," he inquired in a casual, conversational way, "how does it feel to have broken vows sworn on blood and flesh before the Iron Heart of Khali-Zoramatoth the Lord of Chaos? Do you not fear Phul and Hagith and Oeh the Spirit of the Sun? Do your night dreams not echo with terrible visions of the Scarlet Lake or the Black Eye of Ygg that reads what is written on the heart of each man? Do you not quail in terror from the Pentacle of Lead and do not the grim names of Aratron and Bethor and Cassiel ring in your ears . . .?"

Color drained from the old enchanter's face, leaving a sickly greenish white. His eyes bugged wide in sheer horror and with one palsied and clawlike hand he drew a Sign in midair between himself and Thane. It glowed faintly and hung motionless as a whorl of vapor. Thane spilled a drop of wine on the table-top and traced a countersigil with his fingertip. It hissed and bubbled, snapping with blue sparks.

"Aquiel over Silchard," the swordsman observed gently, "and Phaleg must bow before the Green Lion of Zarzamathool, as it is written in Aptolcater the Book of Power . . ."

The glowing Sign broke suddenly, and dispersed before the blue radiance of the countersigil.

The old sorceror from Yoth Zembis staggered away from the table, knocking over his chair, and stumbled through the throng while Thane laughed heartily. And, rubbing out the glowing sigil with one hand, he settled back to finish his wine.

The frozen mood of the Inn relaxed. Men moved and talked and laughed again, but carefully refrained from so much as looking in the direction of the tall, red-headed warrior with the two swords at his side. Thus, at his leisure, Thane finished the flacon of mint wine—dropped an iridium *dahler* on the spark-charred tabletop, and rose to his feet.

He went over to the purple-curtained booth and tore the hangings aside.

At a table sat a man fully as tall as himself, and clothed in fabulous raiment worth a Prince's ransom. From throat to wrist to heel he was dressed in crystal cloth that shimmered like iridescent mist and was spun only by the wise, sad-eyed Arachnidae of Algol IV. A great radium ruby from Xulthoon smouldered like a live coal in one lobe, pulsing like the beatings of a crimson living heart.

This man was the victim of a rare ailment. His face and skin were white as milk, and he wore a thick mane of snow-white, silk-fine hair. He was an albino, with eyes like pink rubies, and his face was singularly repulsive, devoid of eyelashes or eyebrows, handsome in its classic regularity of features, but rendered unspeakably hideous due to its dead-white coloration.

A second radium ruby glowed on the forefinger of his strong white hand.

Before him was a beaker of cut crystal, filled with the fiery purple liquor the vintners of Valtomé distill from their musky-scented wine apples.

Thrust through a jewel-encrusted girdle was an electric whip, its supple handle glinting and winking with ice blue diamonds.

Thane smiled without humor.

"I fear I distressed your tame wizard somewhat . . . although not as drastically as your Chadorian. Sorry."

The white-skinned man, who had not moved a muscle from the moment Thane tore the purple curtains aside, smiled arrogantly.

"No matter," he said in a soft voice. "Such servants can be bought and sold like animals. I am looking for a truly exceptional man. Yourself, for example. To such a man as you, I can offer for a simple service a price almost beyond . . ."

"I am not for sale," Thane said with a pleasant smile. "I suggest you try one of the alleys leading off the Forum of Ashlak. You will find there boys perfumed and gilded to suit even your epicene tastes—Prince Chan."

One white hand twitched in a convulsive spasm of rage, and the weird pink eyes flashed.

.."*You dare . . . ?*"

"Thane of the Two Swords has dared many things, my pretty Prince. Come, are there no youths left unsullied in all your world of Shimar, that you must venture into the stews of Zotheera?"

"We have never met. How then do you know me?"

Thane shrugged. "You wear your ear gem after the fashion of the Dragon Stars. And none but a Planetary Prince could afford a suit of Arachnidaen crystal cloth. I have hunted sea bears on the shores of the white seas of Shimar, and know her Prince is the only —*albino*—in the Cluster. And I have heard somewhat of his peculiar sensual tastes—"

Prince Chan stiffened and his ruby eyes glazed with a curious film.

"Indeed, you dare much . . . perhaps, too much," he said in a remote, whispering voice. One strong white hand twitched toward the hilt of his jeweled electric whip and his white lips tightened in a chill grimace.

Thane said in an easy, conversational voice:

"Before you can touch that whip, I can break your arm in three places. But if you care to gamble on the chance that I am bluffing, go ahead. Your Chadorian gave me a disappointing workout—he folded too quickly and I would enjoy a bit more exercise."

The Prince relaxed with a visible effort.

"I would like to test your much-vaunted speed," he said, smiling, "and it would afford me . . . much

pleasure . . . to chastise you. But you are too valuable to my needs for me to afford this kind of self-indulgence. I will give you"—he continued, in the same
easy tone—"one million pieces of gold if you will
enter my service for three days."

Thane blinked incredulously. That kind of wealth
could set up a wandering spaceman for the rest of his
life!

"How about—*two* million?" he countered.

Chan of Shimar blinked up at him with weird pink
eyes inscrutable in a masklike face.

"Very well," he said softly.

Thane shook his head in reluctant admiration.

"I yield to none," he laughed, "in having a high estimate of my own abilities. But for a price like that
you could hire an entire army of mercenaries . . . and
I cannot but feel there is nothing one man could do,
even if he be Thane of the Two Swords, that an army
could not!"

Prince Chan's white face was inscrutable.

"Let me be the judge of that," he said. "Do you—ac-
cept the price?"

Thane smiled down at him.

"I would not work for a pink-eyed pig like you for
an hundred times the price," he said sweetly.

Chan's mask broke—his mouth writhed uncontrolla-
bly. One hand clamped to his girdle—but Thane had
him by the throat. He had moved like chain lightning,
and his thumb sank into a clump of ganglia beneath
the Prince's ear in a numbing pressure. His motor-
nerves momentarily paralyzed by the golden swordsman's grip, the Prince slumped back helplessly, panting with fury.

"That's better," Thane approved. "I have a dislike

for public quarrels—they are so ill bred. And these whips do leave such ugly scars . . ."

"You gutter filth, I'll carve your brain with an electric needle—!" the white-faced man snarled. Foam frothed at the corners of his lips as they worked spasmodically.

"Such temper!" Thane reproved, shaking his red mane. "You might very well cause someone harm in such a mood. Perhaps it would be wise to take away your toys, until you learn to play by the rules?"

He snapped the jewel-studded whip in two, sprinkling the tabletop with minute diamonds. The corded length hissed. Blue sparks snapped from the naked copper strands at its tip as the tiny power pack in the hilt shorted out. Oily black smoke wisped from the ruined whip.

"There, that's better."

Thane doubled up the broken weapon into a ball and tucked it neatly into the cut-crystal beaker of liquor. The Prince helplessly watched with mad, raging eyes.

"Improves the flavor, you'll find," Thane grinned, patting the sides of the beaker. "Adds that certain tang that makes all the difference."

Then he pulled the purple curtain closed again and strode out of the inn called The House of Thirteen Pleasures and into the night that now arched over the City of a Thousand Gods.

The little sorceror returned to find his Master physically recovered from his encounter with Thane, but seething with an ice cold fury.

"Master, what shall we do? This man is too dangerous—perhaps another . . .?"

"There is no other. He alone hath the Jewel of Amzar, as the Time Priest swore—hath it, or knows the secret of its power and can open the Web of the Aealim. It must be he and no other—either by purchase, or by force, or by subterfuge, we must gain his services."

"And—after we are done with him?" the dwarfed sorceror slyly insinuated.

Prince Chan smiled a slow quiet smile.

"He shall die . . . leisurely . . . artistically. I have in mind that death called The Thousand Silver Kisses . . ."

The sorceror's slitted eyes gleamed hotly.

"Once on Yoth Zembis, ere I left the Brotherhood, I saw a man die that death, Master! It took almost a year for him to die . . ."

The Prince rose to his feet, gathering up a cloak of woven gold spun soft as finest silk by a secret process guarded jealously by the Blind Weavers of 61 Cygni IV.

"Come, Druu. We are not finished yet. I have one more weapon in my arsenal, and it is a blade to which no man is proof . . ."

Thane strode through the nighted streets toward the space field where his ship lay berthed. He had thought to sleep at an inn, but now he knew he had enemies in this city of Zotheera, and would sleep more safely in his own craft. He was thinking of this Prince Chan and pondering what possible reason or purpose the albino could have for trying to hire his services at such fantastic prices . . . when something soft and warm and rounded collided with him.

He looked down at the girl who wrapped slim arms

about his neck and stared up at him with eyes of dim-
mest shadowy purple now haunted with a spectral
fear.

"Help me ... *please* ... help me ..." she
cried. And Thane had only time enough to observe
that she was naked save for a hovering veil of colored smoke and a great moony opal clasped at the
lobe of one small ear.

In the next second five men in the long, voluminous
cloth robes of the Desert Warriors were pointing Dai-
koonish swords at him. One snarled from a swarthy
snarling face adorned with feud paint stripes of red
and green on his lank cheeks:

"So you had an accomplice, eh, wench? Outworlder
—either give us the Seven Gold Dragons, or the slut.
And, in either case, prepare to die—!"

The steel point flashed toward Thane's naked
throat.

3 THE JEWEL OF AMZAR

WITH ONE LITHE catlike motion, Thane spun on his heel—thrust the girl behind him in a whirl of colored smokes—and, crossing his arms across his middle, whipped his two swords from their scabbards.

On one blade he caught and turned the Desert Warrior's thrust. As it flashed over his shoulder, he drew a line of leaking scarlet down the man's swarthy cheek.

Red blood dribbled into his scraggly beard, and mingled with the feud paint on his cheek.

The five warriors recoiled—disconcerted at the swiftness of his motions—and spread out in a crescent facing him.

Thane stood in the center of this half ring of men. Save for them, the alley was empty. Greasy cobbles glinted, catching the faint golden moonrise. Walls of ancient, crumbling brick rose sheer to either hand.

He stood spread-legged, his legs bent slightly at the knees, vast blue cloak thrust back over each shoulder so as not to encumber his arms. The two swords gleamed in his hands. They were long scimitars of ion-treated steel from his home world.

The first Desert Warrior sprang forward, cursing, his rapier flashing for Thane's throat.

One scimitar smashed his blade aside. The second laid open his throat, and he fell forward in a gush of blood and died with a curse on his lips.

The other four closed in with flashing swords. Steel rang on steel in a clashing metal music. This lithe, long-legged golden panther of a man was something new in the experience of the nomad swordsmen. He fought like a tiger, his two glittering blades flashing in rhythm. One man staggered back clutching a stump that gushed forth a flood of scarlet where only a moment before a strong capable hand had been. The second fell screaming as Thane's steel bit through bone and sinew deep into his heart.

Thane's ringing laughter rose above the clash of steel, the hoarse oaths, the shrill cries of the wounded. The girl watched with wide, astonished eyes. His swords moved almost too swiftly for the eye to follow their strokes. But in a moment each blade's tip left an arc of crimson droplets on the air.

The third swordsman stumbled back from the battle, a terrible red smear where his face had been, a broken sword falling from palsied, strengthless fingers to ring like an iron bell on the cobbles.

The fourth sought to strike at Thane's scarlet head, but the swordsman ducked and his blade speared deep into his opponent's chest. The nomad dropped his sword and gaped at the blade that protruded from his breast like a new limb, suddenly produced by magic. He plucked at the hilt with a nerveless hand. Then his knees gave way and he too crumpled to the oily cobbles.

Thane turned to the fifth and last, but he had fled,

his face working with terror, racing out of the alley as if some demon from the Pits of Torment glibbered at his heels.

The golden swordsman bent over the fourth assailant who was gasping out his life on the cobbles. The nomad glared up at him with glazing eyes, his gaudy-colored feud marks harshly brilliant against a leaden-colored face beaded with glistening sweat.

"You . . . devil . . . we'll get . . . the Jewel . . . yet . . . *ahhhhhhhhh —*"

Thane set a booted heel against his face and bent, drawing his scimitar from the corpse. He wiped both blades clean on the robes of the fallen, settled them back in their twin scabbards, and turned to the girl who had been the cause of all this.

She observed that he was not even breathing hard, although he had just killed four men within half that many minutes.

Thane looked at her from cool, admiring eyes. She was an exquisite young thing, slim and softly rounded, her small sweet breasts and creamy arms and long, slender legs gleaming like polished ivory behind the dim veil of opal-tinted perfumed smoke that clung about her, confined by the surface tension of a molecular binding field.

"Now, girl, what was all this about?" he demanded. "I have just killed men—and, for my peace of mind if nothing else, I like to know why. *Speak!*"

Her immense purple eyes were dimly bright in the pale luminous oval of her young face. He noted absently that her hair was a soft cloud of shadowy, silken darkness wherein were woven small copper bells that chimed softly whenever she moved. Small she was, aye, hardly coming up to his shoulder. And fair almost beyond belief . . .

"They . . . they are warriors in the service of Shastar of the Red Moon," she panted, her young breasts rising and falling rapidly—and distractingly—beneath the veil of scented vapor. "I am a dancer at the Inn of the Nine Jackals . . . one of Shastar's chieftains took a fancy to me . . . and I repulsed him."

Thane regarded her skeptically.

"When did a dancing girl ever say 'no' to a Desert Chief?" he demanded. She smiled faintly.

"I am freeborn, and choose the man I like. I am not for sale," she said with a flash of spirit. He laughed.

"Well said! And a standard I, too, hold dear. But please continue—"

She shrugged small creamy shoulders.

"There is little more that I can say, Out worlder . . . this chieftain took my refusal badly . . . he swore to have me with or without my leave . . . and when I refused again, he claimed loudly I had stolen the treasure of his Clan . . ."

"Seven gold dragons?"

She nodded.

"And do you have these dragons?"

Again, that fragile ghost of a smile.

"This veil of smoke—the 'costume' in which I dance —barely hides me. Do *you* see golden dragons?" she asked in a faintly mocking tone.

He tossed back his scarlet mane in a hearty laugh.

"Gods, girl, all I see is a bit of very fair young flesh—too fair, in truth, for a heavy-handed Desert Chief! But now that these men are slain—all save the one that fled—what do you do?"

"I . . . I don't know. I cannot return to the Inn, for

the Chief will know where to seek me ... I
have ... *nowhere* to go ... !"

Thane silenced her with a suddenly lifted hand.

"What is it?" she whispered, her face pale in the
dense gloom of the alley.

"*Sh!* A gang of mounted men coming—this way.
Some ten or a dozen of them—"

"I hear nothing ..."

"Nevertheless, they are there."

"What shall we—do?"

Thane frowned, grey eyes roaming about restlessly.

"If we could get to the space field, we would be
safe, for my ship is there. But—curse the luck!—they
are between us and the field ... well, there's no
help for it and we must do the best we can, and trust
to the Lord Shalakh for good fortune. Come!"

"Which way—?"

He grinned: "*Up!*"

Thane sprang to the top of the wall with a supple
bound that would have made the fortune of any acro-
bat who could equal it. Then he dropped flat, extending an arm, and caught her small white hand in his,
drawing her up after him. They crouched together
atop the wall as a gang of riders thundered up
through the alley's mouth, long robes belling out behind them and bare swords flashing in the light of
Daikoon's fourth moon, which had just risen. They
were mounted on slim, long-legged reptiles called
zimdars, bred in the marshes of Gondilon. There were
eleven of them, armed with naked steel and nerve
guns. Their leader, masked behind a cowl of crimson
silken stuff, bore an electric whip and a long-barreled
lightning gun.

They rode up to the fallen men whom Thane had

killed. Several dismounted to examine the bodies for life; the others rode the length of the alley, presuming the swordsman and the girl had escaped in that direction.

Thane touched the girl's arm.

"Come," he said softly.

"Which way?"

"Over the roofs. If we can make it to the edge of the space field, we are safe—"

Taking her hand, he led her along the wall and then up to the roof of the nearest building. They went through the ghostly moons' light on silent feet, their way made perilous by the shifting fourfold shadows. The four moons were orbs of weirdly differing hues aloft in a sky of purple velvet.

Domes and minarets rose about them to either side. When they came to the further end of this building's roof, they stopped short. A torch-lit street gaped below them. The edge of the next building's roof seemed to lie a full league away.

The girl shrank against him faintly.

"How do we get across . . . that?" she gasped.

He grinned recklessly, teeth flashing white in the dimness.

"Only one way, girl. We *jump*."

Her eyes flared wide. Her lips began to form a startled word, but he bent and took her up into his arms.

"No words, now," he cautioned. "Cling to my back —that's the way, one arm around my neck, the other across my chest beneath my shoulder—like so. Now—"

"We'll be *killed*—"

"Be silent, or I will leave you here and escape all alone," he said sternly, and she quieted meekly.

He paced back the full distance, measuring the gap

with cold grey eyes. Long steely sinews coiled and tensed like powerful springs in his rangy legs.

It would not be an easy thing . . . the roof opposite was of overlapping tiles, and it sloped down to a level lip . . . his timing must be precise, and the slightest error in equipoise could hurl them into the cobbled street far below. At his shoulder, he could feel the girl's panting breath and the muffled drumming of her heart.

He ran to the roof's edge and sprang like a great cat. His body jackknifed in midair—then straightened out, arms stretched to their fullest.

The tiles came up and caught him the full length of his body, almost driving the air out of his lungs. At the same instant, his clutching hands slipped on the slick tiles—slid—his feet went over the edge and they swung in empty space. But his hands clamped like a vise on the lip of the roof, and he clung. His grip was so intense that the glazed tiles *crunched* under finger pressure.

Taking a deep breath, he levered himself up until he was crouching on the level ledge on all fours. Everything swam in a giddy mist of vertigo—then, with an effort of iron will, he gained control again.

Safe!

But it was not a feat he would care to attempt again, even without the girl clinging to his back.

He remembered, with a surge of warm admiration, that even in mid-leap she had not panicked, nor screamed.

From that point, they went on along the roof edge and over the next building and around a narrow ledge that circled a great fat-bellied dome whose copper rondure was green with verdigris, and thence across a long flat roof to the edge of the street that faced the old space field. There they lay on their bellies and peered out the crenelations of the battlement.

The field was flat and dark, save for the silvery glimmer of uplifting needle-prowed hulls washed with the radiance of the four moons.

"Curse the luck!" he growled.

Some dozen or fifteen Desert Warriors mounted on swift-pacing reptilian steeds, prowled the length of the street bordering the field. They bore long-snouted laser rifles that could burn through an unshielded man at two hundred paces.

"What shall we do?" the girl whispered. He shrugged. She rose on her white elbows and peered out through the crenelation. The wall that encompassed the city swept in a black rampart beyond the further limits of the field, broken by the Gate of the Star Ships.

"Perhaps . . ." she faltered.

"Go on, lass," he grinned. "If you've an idea, speak it out. I'm in the mood for wild schemes!"

She pointed to their right.

"If we could go that way, and out of the city . . . by the Caravan Gate at the end of this street . . . perhaps we could go back around the city and come in by the field gate from the other side," she said. "I shouldn't think they'd have warriors outside the city, too!"

He rubbed his chin thoughtfully.

"Well, why not?" he said. He got to his feet, crouching a little so as not to be spotted above the battlements, and went along the front of the building to the corner. Then, turning, he beckoned the girl to follow. When she came up to him, he turned and grinned at her, white teeth flashing in the gloom, went over the edge and dropped feet first into the alley.

One of the mounted warriors was riding by directly below. Thane's booted heels caught him on the shoulders and knocked him sprawling in a whirl of woolen robes. The zimdar, suddenly deprived of its rider, bucked and reared in alarm, its parrot beak champing, voicing a shrill hiss of fear. Thane caught its bridle and—with a surge of powerful shoulders—brought the beast to its knees.

The warrior groggily came to his knees, one brown hand groping for a weapon in his belt.

Still holding the reins, Thane lashed out with one booted foot. He caught the warrior full in the throat, snapping his head back with an audible crack of splintering vertebrae. The dead man fell back against the cobbles, his swarthy, bearded face frozen in an expression of stunned surprise. Thane relieved him of rifle and whip.

"*Jump!*" he called softly to the girl above, and caught her slight form easily in his strong arms.

All of this had only taken moments. The attack on the lone warrior had not been noticed. Thane sprang astride the zimdar, which hissed like a steampipe, and drew the girl up behind him. Then he guided the reptile out into the dimly lit street and, keeping to the shadowed side under an arcade, they paced swiftly toward the gate at the street's end. By some miracle, they were not seen.

Her soft body warm against his naked shoulder, the girl whispered in his ear.

"I never thought you'd make that leap between the buildings!"

He grunted. "I come from a heavy gravity planet; Daikoon is a light metals world with only a fraction of the gravitational field I am accustomed to. Still, it was not a thing I'd care to try every day—I notice you didn't scream!"

She laughed, shakily.

"I was too frightened to scream! But thank the Gods it's over . . ."

The gate, of course, was unguarded—this was Festival Week—and they went through it into the flat desert that dreamed in shadow silence under the four moons. He reined the beast to the left and they began to follow the immense curve of the city's wall, when—

The girl gasped: *"Behind us!"*

Looking back over his shoulder, Thane saw a score of mounted warriors boiling out of the Caravan Gate and loping after them across the moonlit sands. Either they had been seen leaving the city after all, or the corpse of this zimdar's rider had been discovered only seconds after they had ridden out into the street.

"Hang on," he said grimly. He jerked the zimdar's head around with a powerful surge of muscles, and thudded his heels into its scaly sides. Rearing back on its haunches, the reptile launched forward into a swift, loping stride. It flew like the wind, long snaky neck stretched forward, and great splay feet pacing the sand with incredible speed. The pursuit shrank into the distance against the great clotted mass of darkness that was the city of Zotheera.

He guided the beast straight out into the desert, but had little hopes of outdistancing the riders behind. Their mount was a superb racer, but he carried a double load and this first surge of breathtaking speed would soon be over as the extra weight began to tell on him.

And as they rode, Thane's thoughts were busy with a nagging problem. There was a curious discrepancy in the girl's story: she said the warriors were after her over a matter of Seven Gold Dragons . . . but the man he had killed back in the alley had gasped out something about "the Jewel" with his last breath.

Were these men actually after *him?*

Was the girl a front—or even an ally of the warriors?

Were they after . . . *the Jewel of AMZAR?*

Bent forward over the zimdar's massive shoulders, he used all his skill to coax the last possible atom of speed out of the beast.

Their only hope lay in getting out of sight of the pursuit before their steed began to lose speed. Then they could—with luck—double back into the city, entering through one or another of its eleven gates.

He goaded the sleek zimdar on ruthlessly, mercilessly, to the last erg of energy in its muscles.

And all the time he pondered grimly. The slim, fair girl with purple eyes who clung to his broad shoulders . . . was she what she seemed . . . or was she the most cunning of all possible traps?

4 ILLARA OF THE PURPLE EYES

FIVE MOONS rode high in the velvet sky, glowing like goblin lanterns, softly golden green, palest pink, faint yellow, dim azure and ashen silver.

By their wavering, five fold luminance, the undulating sands became a land of enchantment. They rode through a sea of many-colored shadows, through a maze of softly rounded hills of silken sand that whispered under the pacing feet of the great reptile to whose scaly back they clung.

A mile or two beyond Zotheera of the Thousand Gods, the level sands rose into a world of dunes. Within moments they lost sight of their enemies. The moonlit desert was magically transformed into a maze of shallow hills of gleaming sand and shadow-haunted vales that curved and wandered between.

In no time they were completely lost. But, as they had no way of telling whether they had lost the pursuit or not, they continued on.

The stars, from whose positions Thane might have read direction, were all but invisible in the dazzling radiance of the five moons of Daikoon. And these moons themselves so swiftly curved across the sky, that in the first hour the nearer of the five had crossed the heavens, vanished below the horizon, and risen again.

In time, the zimdar wearied.

Its speed slacked. Its parrot beak gasped for breath. Foam dribbled down its scaly jaws. Thane let the reins hang loose, and allowed the weary reptile to find its own pace.

They rode on without speaking.

Hills of coral pink rock rose before them, carved by millions of years of abrasive wind into fantastic peaks and pagodas, like the weird ramparts of some city of the gnomes or kobolds, crested with grotesque turrets and minarets under a violet sky filled with racing, many-colored moons.

The black mouth of a cave yawned in one wind-sculpted salmon pink cliff.

He reined the weary zimdar to a halt, and they dismounted. They went into the cavern and found it untenanted—but not for long.

Thane was removing the saddle bags and the girl, whose exhaustion was obvious, was searching through them for food or drink, when an unexpected visitor came sledding down the slope of the sand dune opposite the cave's mouth.

Thane had heard of the sand dragons of Daikoon, but had never before seen one. A long, supple reptillan body, mustard yellow, with a ridge of horny spines along the back, from the center of its brow to the tip of its barbed tail. Six legs armed with dagger-sharp claws and webbed with tough membranes to support it over the sea of sand.

The girl screamed from behind him.

The sand dragon arched its long snaky neck, hunting the sound. Eyes like balls of green flame blazed in the shifting shadows.

Thane went forward to meet it alone, the two swords gleaming in his hands. He wished now he had a lightning gun, or at least something more powerful than the little laser pistol in his pouch which was no better than a toy and whose bolt would only tease the dragon, since he had expended most of its small charge on the Chadorian back at the inn.

It saw him and charged.

The sand dragon slithered across the slope on its flat sledlike belly, propelled by the surge of its tail, and the six short legs. Its neck lunged toward Thane's head. For an instant he looked into a gaping maw lined with glistening fangs.

Then he sprang lightly to one side, scimitars slashing. One blade caught the monster at the base of the neck—the other slashed into its tender snout.

O!!!!!!! Squalling with fury and pain, it reared, striking at him with razory claws. Thane sprang backward. The dragon lunged to follow him, and he struck with the scimitars again.

The yellow dragon was mailed in a tough, leathery hide inches thick. And beneath this mail, a sheath of rubbery muscles slid. If he could catch it with the keen edge of his swords, the ion-bathed steel might—just might—cut through. But the monstrous lizard thing was in constant motion, and his blades turned on the sleek hide, making only shallow slashes.

He avoided its lunge with another adroit side step, and swung with all his strength at the nearest paw.

A lucky stroke! He sheared the limb cleanly through. Clutching convulsively at empty air, the severed member thudded wetly into the brown sand and the stump spewed a bubbling froth of green reptilian gore.

The thing screamed with an ear-splitting cry of agony.

The snout swung toward him again, the fanged mouth opening and closing, champing with fury. Venomous saliva leaked down in dribbles of slime. He swung at this tender snout—he had hurt it there once —and if he could get the eyes—

But he mistook his footing in the sand, and lurched. Snapping jaws closed over one scimitar and tore it from his grasp.

He rolled aside from reach of its scrabbling claws.

Fangs rasped and grated on the steel, and the dragon spat the sword aside.

Now he had only one blade left.

He met its charge squarely, without dodging aside. It reared up before him, and he drove the scimitar's point directly into the broad, flat chest. The impact of its weight on the blade drove him back, sinking his booted heels into the soft sand.

But the dragon's breast was shielded with immense flat sliding muscles. The sword only sank three or four inches in—and stuck.

Before he could drag it out, one buffeting paw smashed him aside as a child knocks a rag doll flying. He smacked into the dune with his shoulder, slightly stunned, but staggered to his feet again moments later.

The dragon was threshing and squalling with pain and rage, pounding the sand furiously with its flat tail, raising a storm of dust. The sword protruded from the center of its chest, but it only impeded the beast, and had not penetrated deeply enough to cripple it. The paw stump, he saw with dazed eyes, had already stopped bleeding. The thing was almost un-killable!

And now he faced it with bare hands.

It saw him and came after him again, wriggling up the shallow slope of the dune. The crippled paw spoiled its coordination, and it slid, scrabbling wildly, to the foot of the dune again without reaching him.

Looking around for a weapon, Thane saw the girl come out of the cave where she had crouched during the battle. She was running to the left and something black and ropy was coiled in her small white hand.

The electric whip he had taken from the dead rider!

"Here!" he called.

She ran to the foot of the dune, well around the curve from the slope up which the dragon was strug-gling to climb, and flung the whip toward him.

He caught it by the handle, just as the shrieking lizard came up to him. Thumbing the power pack to life, he snapped out the whip's long length.

It curled around the dragon's throat with a crack-ling discharge. Foot long blue sparks of electric fire cracked from its stinging tip.

The monster screamed! He recoiled the whip as the creature lurched back, tail beating the loose, lion-col-ored sand. The electric whip had burned long black scars about the dragon's throat.

He slashed it again, searing it terribly across the breast wherefrom his sword still protruded. The air was hot with the sharp smell of ozone and the nau-seous stench of burned flesh. The shadowy gloom was weirdly lit with jagged waves of blue fire that slith-ered the length of the whip as it sang and snapped, coiling like a rope of fire around the writhing reptile.

For a time he managed to keep the thing at bay.

The whip crackled. Sparks snapped and sizzled. The beast made ferocious attempts to get at him with hungry jaws and slashing feet, but he eluded it narrowly, just barely managing to keep his footing on the dune crest in the loose, rustling sand.

And then he caught it full across the naked eyes.

The dragon went mad.

Its empty eye sockets charred black pits that oozed a fetid slime, it exploded in a blind frenzy of insane fury, tearing at its own seared flesh in mindless fury. In a spasm of incredible rage, it tore out its own throat with iron hard, dagger sharp claws. A great gout of green snake blood gushed from the horrible gaping wound to bathe its entire chest.

The arched, weaving, blinded head sank.

Still twitching feebly, it stiffened and slid slowly down the slope of the dune to the base. Sand slid down, half-covering it.

The flat tail slapped at the sand for a moment, then a long tremor went through its length and it sagged bonelessly and was dead.

In an aching, utter silence, broken only by the wind sighing over the sandy dune crests, Thane came slowly down the slope. He retrieved both swords and cleaned them by thrusting them into the sand, and replaced them in the twin scabbards.

He felt suddenly very weary.

The girl came up to him sobbing breathlessly and came into the circle of his arms and he held her; she was small and soft and warm.

"Thanks for remembering the whip," he said.

And his head bent, his mouth meeting hers in a long hard kiss. Suddenly, his tired body was thrillingly aware of the live, bare length of her. The fragrance of her cloak of scented vapor was heady in his nostrils, and the many tiny copper bells woven through her long black hair chimed sweetly.

She clung to him, nestling in the strong circle of his bare arms, after he had broken off the kiss.

"I've never asked your name," he said.

"Illara," she said huskily.

"I am called Thane of the Two Swords," he said.

She lifted the pale sweet oval of her face to his to be kissed again.

"Love me, Thane," she said. And the thunder of his drumming pulse rose to match hers as he claimed her eager lips, and he lost himself in the warmth and softness of her there in the shifting, many-colored light of the five drifting moons.

After a long time, she slept, curled up in his great blue cloak on the rocky floor of the cave. The zimdar's saddle bags had contained a meal of sorts: dried figs from Faraz and some salted strips of meat wrapped up in oiled cloth, and a skin bottle of sour green wine from Shazar. And there was even a garment of voluminous, tawny-colored wool, in which she had clothed herself against the chill air of the desert night.

They had eaten and drunk, and now she slept while he sat sprawled comfortably on the piled saddle bags at the mouth of the cave, keeping watch.

The colored moons went up and down the sky like paper lanterns drifting in the wind. After a time he closed his eyes against their distracting and hypnotic rhythms, and, in a while, he slept.

He had done much that day and even his superb

body could not forever sustain itself against fatigue. He slept like a dead man while the moons went down the sky and the east paled into the stupendous glory of the desert dawn.

One by one, the Three Suns of Daikoon floated up in the east and the cloudless sky brightened before them into a fantastic glory of gold and crimson. The purple sky paled into a hot, luminous grey that swiftly deepened into rich azure.

The long, long night was over and day had come.

And Thane was rudely awakened by a booted foot that thudded into his ribs.

He opened his eyes and saw that the cave was filled with grinning men.

"On your feet, dog!" said the one whose ugly little laser pistol was pointed directly at his heart—

5 SHASTAR OF THE RED MOON

THEY HERDED Thane and the frightened girl out of the cave, disarming and binding him. He made no reply to the coarse jests and rough treatment he received, but maintained an impassive and stoical calm. It rankled Thane that he had been caught offguard, and that there was nothing he could do about it. Even his rather unusual powers were helpless, while he was held at gun point.

Once out on the sands, he looked up and saw the ship from which their captors had descended. It was a giant cigar-shaped cylinder of sleek, glinting steel against the dawn sky, hovering like a motionless cloud on gravity-resisting pressor beams. The sight of it took his breath away: in these degenerate times following the collapse of the Carina Empire, technology had lapsed and much science had been forgotten. No ships were built these days; no one knew how. You simply used the ships the age-dead Imperials had made, and when even their tireless engines wore out at last after centuries, you did without. But such ships as the one aloft were rare and seldom seen: Thane knew it at once for an Imperial battlewagon, and his

43

warrior's heart sang at the sheer beauty and perfection of it . . .

One of the bearded Desert Warriors struck him roughly.

"Turn around, Offworlder dog!"

He turned without speech. Resistance was futile. He could but wait, and watch for a chance . . .

They strapped Thane and Illara into paragravity harnesses, and leashed to the leader of the band, they drifted up into the clear morning sky like spirits. All the warriors wore such equipment under their flowing robes that belled and billowed about them, flapping like the wings of huge ungainly birds. This, too, was a bit of rare ancient craft. Thane wondered who the chief of their captors was, who had such magnificent gear . . .

The ship swelled above them, filling the sky, darkening the Three Suns. An airlock opened in its belly and they floated in. The leader of the Warriors tugged them by their leash and they floated down to a steel deck. More warriors swarmed about them, grinning at Illara's beauty half-veiled in the stolen robe of tawny wool they had found in the saddle bags. They took off the harnesses and led them from the vast echoing hold into a ship's corridor.

Here all was humming machinery and winking lights, and long walls and corridors and endless rooms of glistening, ageless metal. Whoever owned this well-preserved relic, he kept it in superb condition: not a fleck of rust or a single example of disorder or clutter could Thane see.

They came into a great hall.

Once it had been a storage compartment, but that was centuries ago. Now it was transformed into a scene of barbaric might and magnificence. Tattered battle ensigns and golden tapestries adorned the steel-plated walls. The deck was carpeted with priceless rugs and rare furs. At one end of the hall rose a dais of rich marble, bearing a throne of spicewood covered all over with thin plates of beaten gold. Behind it against the wall was a giant banner—a sheet of dead black silk charged with a mighty crescent of scarlet.

On the throne sat Shastar of the Red Moon. It could be none other than he. A giant of a man, taller even than Thane, burly as a bull, with a flaming golden beard, hook nose, and scowling black brows. His huge frame was wrapped in a cloak of silver furs, and beneath the furs, a long-skirted suit of scale armor glinted in the light of flickering torches, black scales as the body of some monstrous serpent. He looked rapacious, intelligent, and strong.

They brought Thane and Illara to the foot of the marble dais. Illara they hurled to her knees, but they could not make Thane kneel: he stood like a statue of cold bronze, staring impassively at Shastar's keen eyes and ignoring the blows of the warriors. After a few moments, Shastar clapped his hands and gestured them away.

"Enough! Let him stand, if he wishes it."

They desisted from their buffets, and stepped away, leaving Thane alone before their monarch. Shastar brooded down at him with frowning brows, his bearded chin resting on one palm.

"How are you named, swordsman?" he asked at last.

"Thane."

"A Zhayan, by your hair. Well, then, swordsman—do you know why you're here?"

"A matter of seven gold dragons," Thane said quietly. "About which I know nothing whatever."

"Nothing, eh?" Shastar grunted. "By the Beard of Arnam, we'll find the truth of that! Doubtless yon pretty lass has them hidden somewhere . . . Thane . . . Thane . . . where have I heard of you? Something about—*ah!* Thaxis of the Scarlet Spears—you are Thane of the Two Swords!" he roared, for his keen eye, wandering over Thane's body, had noted the two empty scabbards clipped to Thane's girdle.

"I am. But I thought not my fame had penetrated to these stars," Thane grinned.

Shastar boomed with robust humor. "Ah, but it has, by Zargon's Balance! You are the man who stole the Jewel of Amzar from the temple of the Time Priests on Mnom the Dark World . . . tell me, swordsman, where is this Time Jewel?"

Thane was puzzled, but his bronze face did not show it. He shrugged.

"I do not have it. I know nothing of it—"

"Hah, by Thaxis, Arnam and all the Gods, we'll find the truth in that! That gem is sacred to those that worship the Aealim . . . they'll pay a goodly price to have it back. Listen, swordsman, I'll put aside the matter of the gold dragons: tell me where the gem of Amzar is, and I'll strike off your bonds, and put you down without the walls of Zotheera, alive and unharmed. What say you to that?"

Thane was strongly tempted. It would be an easy matter to reveal what little he knew of the Jewel—but would this Shastar believe his story? It would sound incredible to most ears, and Thane could prove nothing of what he could tell . . . then, again, his suspicions were aroused. He remembered the dying words of the Desert Warrior he had slain in rescuing Illara: he, too, had mentioned the Jewel . . . strange! There was more to all this than seemed obvious . . . and somewhere in all of this, Prince Chan was involved . . . and—Illara?

He smiled up at Shastar.

"Your offer is a good one, chieftain, but I can't buy my life with what I know of the Time Jewel. What I know can be put in one word: *nothing.*"

Shastar chewed over that in brooding silence for a time, then, abruptly, he gestured to the leader of the men who had captured Thane and the girl.

"Gorshang! Throw this man and the woman into a cell and make sure the fellow is stoutly chained, I distrust him. I have heard strange things of this Zhayan ere now . . . *ho,* you there, run to the bridge and tell old Zugoth to take us home, lively now! And when you come back, bring wine with you—all this talking has given me a thirst!"

They bound him to the wall, spreadeagled, his arms and legs clamped with steel bands. The girl they did not bother to bind, but simply cuffed her into a corner and went out, slamming the great steel door behind them. Thane was happy to see they had left a jug of something drinkable, and some spiced, salty meat.

He comforted Illara's tears with heartening words, and soon she dried her eyes and came to him. At his urging she ate and drank and held meat for him to eat of it, as his hands were bound. It was sharply salted and made him thirsty, and when he drank from the jug he was surprised to discover it contained a rich purple brandy, heady and strong and bracing. He drank deeply of it, feeling it send warmth through his limbs, relaxing him.

"Thane, what is this Jewel the Lord Shastar wants?" she asked, after he had eaten. "Can you give it to him?"

Between gulps from the pitcher which she held for him, he said, "I don't know why he wants the damned thing, but I can't give it to him."

"But what *is* it? And what are the Time Priests?" she asked.

"The Time Priests worship the Aealim, the Children of The Fire Mist, and they worship them by means of the Jewel, their talisman," he said. She mutely urged him to continue.

"The Children of The Fire Mist came from Aea at the beginning of time. Aea is some region or dimension beyond the Universe of Stars, I don't know much about it. These Aelim are called 'the Time Wizards' by their priests: they are not really Gods, but a race of beings who are supposed to have inhabited the Galaxy before man arose; they're called Time Wizards because they are believed to be able to see through time, as it were, to see the past and the present and the future as one continuous scroll. Anyway, they left the Galaxy ages ago, and today they are worshiped by their fanatic sect of Time Priests as divinities."

He drank some more of the fiery brandy.

"Yes? And . . . the Jewel?" the girl prompted.

"That's enough of that stuff, I'll be getting drunk!" he chuckled. "Eh? Well, the Jewel of Amzar is a giant crystal the Aealim left behind; they left a lot of things behind, and the Priests revere these as relics. But the Jewel . . . that's something else again. More than just a huge gem . . . some sort of crystal mechanism maybe . . ."

"What . . . kind of mechanism?"

He shrugged. "I don't know. Something that connects the Time Priests with the Aealim, in some curious way. Some kind of repository for their wisdom . . . or maybe it's more of a storage battery for their weird power over time . . . I don't know."

She lifted the pitcher to his lips again.

"Here, Thane," she urged. "Drink some more; those clamps are cutting into your arms, and your muscles must ache from that uncomfortable position."

He shook his head stubbornly, tousling his crimson mane. "No more. I've drunk enough. You rest now; sleep if you can. I've got to think . . ."

The warship rose from its orbit around Daikoon the Desert World and hurtled off into the darkness of space toward the Red Moon where Shastar reigned. Some time after leaving the plane of the ecliptic, the craft transposed from normal space into an artificial universe of pure mathematical paradox, the *Interplenum,* where a ship could outrace light hundreds of times over.

Shastar's Moon circled a dead planet called Phiolanthe, whose primary was an aging, cooled Red Dwarf named Sardane, and this system lay some eleven lightyears Rimward of Daikoon. Daikoon, Phiolanthe, and other worlds among the Near Stars such as Argion, Xulthoom, Zha, Scather, Shimar and Mnom the Dark World of the Time Priests, all belong to the Wyvern Cluster of the Orion Spur. This outjutting "spur" of stars is midway along the Carina-Cygnus Arm of the First Galaxy and it was in this arm that the ancient Carina Empire was regnant nine centuries ago.

And here, countless ages before the first Earthmen spread from the legendary Mother World to found the Empire, once ruled the mysterious Aealim.

On the bridge of his mighty battlewagon, Shastar brooded over these ancient matters, and solaced himself with a beaker of purple liquor distilled from the wine-apples of Valthomé. He scowled absently at the screens and the busy men before them, engaged in piloting the ship through that nonexistent abstraction called the Interplenum. He was worried . . . this Thane of the Two Swords was a strong and bold warrior, and he had a head on his shoulders and a reputation for being able to use it. Shastar wondered how long they would be able to keep him off balance . . .

A chime rang somewhere in the dimness of the bridge. A warrior strode up to him and saluted, murmuring in his ear. Shastar grunted, nodded, gestured the man away, and turned in his massive swivelchair to the board, thumbing a switch.

The screen lit up and a face appeared.

It was a strong, handsome face, classically regular of feature but hideous due to its utter whiteness of skin, and cold eyes like pink rubies.

The face of Prince Chan of Shimar.

"How does the work progress?" Chan asked in his cold, precise voice. Shastar shrugged, moodily.

"It goes forward, Highborn. Slowly."

"What did he say—did you ask him about the Jewel? We rehearsed the scene . . ."

Shastar grunted. "I asked him. He says he knows nothing of the Time Jewel."

Chan's cold eyes burned from the screen.

"You promised him life and liberty?" he probed.

Shastar nodded. "He was not impressed. I am, with him. He is a—*man*. Thaxis' Spear, I could love that man! Strong as a God. I would love to see him fight."

Chan smiled icily.

"You may, yet. He fights well. Crippled a bully-boy of mine and nearly drove my dwarf warlock mad . . . what's going on now? Is—"

"The girl's with him, plying him with drink and questions. Maybe she'll get something out of him; I hope so. Gods, I hate this filthy business—lies, tricks, spying! Put a sword in my hand, and I am a man. Ask me to play a part like some soft-gutted stage actor and I—*faugh!* I begin to wish I'd never listened to you—and never joined you in this dirty game of yours—"

Chan's smile was like a knife blade, cold and sharp and thin and mirthless.

"—Of *ours*, my dear ally and comrade. And we are better so. We were both after the Time Treasure, you recall—but independently. Together, we make a fine team: you have men and ships; I, the information."

"The information," Shastar acidly reminded him, "is being pried out of the swordsman right now—on *my* ship."

"—By *my* slave girl," Prince Chan said smoothly. "Never forget that you were blundering around searching for the Tower without information concerning it. It was I, my dear ally and comrade, who located that renegade Time Priest and learned of the Jewel of Amzar, the only talisman capable of opening the Web of the Aealim and taking us to the Tower Beyond Time. Without my knowledge, you would still be thundering around the Near Stars hunting for a planet!"

"Yes, yes . . . Still, I sicken of this business and am sorry I ever entered into that agreement of yours," the burly chieftain grunted.

Chan smiled again. His voice was like a probing needle as he spoke: "The Tower Beyond Time contains the treasure of ten million worlds, culled from ten thousand lost ages, by the Children of The Fire Mist who alone of all beings *transcend* time and can travel through it as we through space. Think of that, my ally: such loot as few conquerors ever dared dream of winning—not Cortez, when the gold of the Aztecs lay at his feet—not godlike Alexander, with the loot of Imperial Persia in his hands—not Shandalar the Red when he broke the Carina legions and took the Heartworld—nor his descendant, Drask of the Star Rovers, with the jeweled treasure vaults of Xulthoom the Mist World in his grasp—*no man ever reached for such a prize as we!*"

The chieftain snorted rudely.

"I know nothing of these Aztecs and Persians, and care less! I know ancient pre-Space history is one of the things you toy with, my pretty Prince, but I have no time for such scholarly playthings. As for Drask of the Varkonna . . . as I recall my recent history, he reached too far, didn't he? I seem to recall the White Wizards of Parlion slapped his wrist for him, and that for all his looting of Xulthoom . . . he *died*. Am I correct, Highborn? Or do you only study the long-dead past, not the recently slain?"

Chan was silent.

Then: "Do you wish out of this, chieftain?"

Shastar sighed gustily, and blew out his cheeks.

"No . . . Thaxis' Spear, I am in it too deep to get out. And I want loot as much as any other man. Cut your beam, Prince; I'll let you know what the wench gets out of this Thane . . ."

Chan smiled, and his image faded from the screen. Shastar sat back with a heavy sigh, and guzzled his liquor as if to remove an unpleasant taste from his mouth.

Ahead, the Red Moon loomed ever closer in the scopes.

It was almost time for the next phase of their little comedy. Shastar wondered how Thane would like it . . .

6 ZANGOR THE MIND GLADIATOR

THE OPPORTUNITY Shastar was waiting for came very soon. Some hours after his conversation with Prince Chan, Thane broke free. It happened during his transfer to another cell. Two burly guards unshackled the warrior while a third held a gun on their prisoner. The guards paid but little attention to Illara, which proved a miscalculation. When Thane was released from the wall, one guard approached him with a wrist chain, while the other held him from behind. Illara seized this chance and struck the pistol from his hand.

It clanged on the deck plates and Thane exploded into action.

He drove a booted heel into the shin of the guard who held his wrists from behind—while hurtling himself head-first at the second guard.

Screaming, clutching a shattered leg, one guard fell to the deck writhing with agony.

Thane butted into the belly of the second guard, his head smashing the fellow flat. Air whooshed from the guard's lungs; his face turned a sickly hue and he retched violently. The third guard dove for the deck

54

and came up with the fallen pistol clenched in his fist. Little pig eyes glittered viciously in his swarthy face.

But Thane had snatched up the manacles. Muscles coiling along his bronzed, bare arm, he swung the heavy steel chain like some terrible whip. The first blow shattered the laser's crystal tube to atoms.

The backlash caught the guard across the jowls. Red welts sprang up and his head snapped back from the impact of the cold steel chain. He sagged to the deck, his skull cracked. The guard who had been butted in the stomach started staggering to his feet, one hand clawing at the spiked iron mace clipped to his girdle. Thane rammed a booted foot in his face. Teeth and bones crunched, snapped. Blood spurted as the guard fell back against the further wall of the cell a limp bundle of bruised flesh.

The entire scene had taken place almost instantaneously: bare-handed, Thane had disposed of three armed guards in almost as many seconds. The girl was appalled at the savage ferocity of his fighting skill: he was more of a tiger than a man. He scooped her up, one powerful arm crooked about the small of her back, and shoved her to the cell door, snapping up the fallen mace. He hefted the spiked weapon in his fist appreciatively. A Zhayan scimitar of ion-bathed steel was more to his taste . . . but prison-breakers can't be choosy!

In the hall outside, he paused, seeking direction. The only hope lay in seizing a gravity belt, or stealing a sky sled, and escaping unnoticed from the belly of the giant ship. No one man could possibly hope to conquer a shipful of enemies—

"This way, girl. Careful, now—"

The corridor was empty, a hollow shaft of metal

glinting in the eternal radiance of its age-old illuminants. Down it they fled, boots thudding on the deck plates. Thane cudgeled his wits, striving to remember and retrace the path by which they had been brought here. Still no guards opposed their way.

They came to a round well in the deck, at the juncture of two corridors. Thane gestured curtly to Illara.

"Jump!"

She stared at him as if he were mad. There was no time to waste giving explanations: he seized her slim body up in his arms and sprang into the well. She shrieked, but he muffled her cry with one hard palm.

They fell like a stone, decks flashing past. Then their fall slowed, as if they were sinking through some denser medium than air. Gently as falling leaves, they drifted down.

"The ancients did not use ladders or stairways on ships this gigantic," he explained hurriedly. "They tamed the force of gravity itself and bent it to their uses. . ."

Within seconds they reached the lowest deck, landing lightly as feathers. Leaving the gravity well, Thane led the girl into the mammoth emptiness of the cavernlike hold—and a dozen guards fell upon him.

Hair trigger senses warned him of a trap. He thrust the girl from him so that she might not encumber his arms; whirling on one heel, he lashed out with the iron mace, catching the foremost guard across the cheek and smashing his jaw. A massive body thudded into him, tripping him and bringing him down. He lashed out with both feet, knocking men sprawling. Springing up lithely, he laid the mace along one man's arm, snapping the ulna like a twig. A backhanded blow sent another hurtling back with shattered ribs. Then the flat of a sword thudded against his skull. Sagging to one knee, sight and sense blurring, he laid about him with the vicious mace. Even in his semiconscious condition, his fighting instincts were such that the mace was a fearful weapon which dealt death and crippled.

A booted foot crashed with stunning force into his side, driving the air from his lungs. He caught the foot and twisted it with a terrific surge of strength, feeling tendons strain and snap. Above the ringing in his ears he heard the shrill yelp as the crippled warrior collapsed.

Then his sight cleared. Shaking his head groggily, he staggered to his feet. Gorshang stood a short distance away, grinning at him as he lifted a glittering tube. *A neuronic scrambler!* He flung his body to one side desperately—

Then his mind exploded in a shower of fireworks and he sank into numb darkness.

Thane folded his arms across his deep chest and stared impassively into Shastar's angry visage. The burly chieftain glowered down at him from the dais, surrounded by grinning guards. The neuronic scrambler left no permanent damage. It merely shorted out the nerve circuits in the brain for a time, without harm. Recovery was swift, even from such a massive charge as Thane had experienced: his mind still felt numb and vertiginous. Although the warrior from Zha did not guess it, the device had not been invented as a weapon but rather as an instrument of mercy. The ancient Imperials had used it during surgery as anesthesia.

"So, swordsman, you like to fight, eh?" Shastar rumbled. "Well, why not? We have an hour ahead of us before we berth at my castle . . . how better to pass the time than to watch you fight, eh? What say, lads, shall we summon Zangor to toy with our captive a bit? A little entertainment, eh?"

The men laughed, nudging each other. Thane allowed no slightest flicker of expression to alter the calm mask of his face, but his nerves prickled, wary as a jungle cat. There was a certain intonation to that laughter that he did not like. However, he was confident of his prowess, and knew he could face any opponent, armed with whatever weapon the arsenals of a thousand worlds could hold . . .

They paced off a wide area, ringing it in, leaving Thane alone in the center. While he awaited the coming of their champion, he searched the grinning throng for a glimpse of Illara and finally saw her manacled at the foot of Shastar's throne. From this distance her face was but a white oval in which her enormous purple eyes glowed with terror. He gave her a reassuring smile.

The crowd parted as Zangor shouldered his way through. The two stood looking each other up and down. Zangor was a great hulking brute of a man with a matted chest and apelike arms that dangled nearly to his knees. From his pointed ears and bald skull, sallow, yellowish flesh and cold slitted eyes of emerald fire, Zangor was a Nexian. Naked but for a clout and harness of black leather set with square iron studs, he was an imposing figure of bestial force, his great arms and shoulders solid masses of beefy muscle. But, curiously, he was unarmed. Thane felt his spirits lift: if this were to be merely a wrestling match, he had little fear that he could not defeat even so powerful an opponent. Thanks to his curious powers, he felt confident of victory. But . . . surely Shastar had some other kind of a contest in mind!

The bearded chieftain laughed.

"Take your helmet, Zangor, and teach this edgy youth a thing or two about *fighting* . . ."

A leering grin split Zangor's yellow jowls. He brought forth a curious-shapen helm of glittering silver and crystal, fitting it upon his brows. Small lights glowed to life amid the tangle of instrumentation that adorned the helm . . . and Thane felt the icy wings of terror brush over his bare flesh. *A Nexian . . . of course!*

Zangor was no wrestler. He was one of the dreaded Mind-Gladiators of Nex!

An invisible sledgehammer thudded into Thane's lean belly. He caved in, gasping with the impact, fighting for breath, dimly aware of Illara's shrill scream and the heavy laughter of the men. He fought to stand against the nausea that surged up in his throat, draining his knees of strength.

An invisible steel vise clamped about his brows, crushing his naked brain.

His senses swam in a scarlet fog as he felt his skull creaking before the numbing pressure.

The pressure vanished as swiftly as it had come. He opened his eyes, swaying groggily.

Invisible needles of searing flame pierced his body from all directions, sinking into shoulders, arms, back and thighs. He winced before the intolerable agony.

Then his legs gave way beneath him and the deck rose up and smacked him in the face. Gasping for breath in the numb valleys between peaks of pain, he clung to the cold plates as a drowning man clings to a raft in stormy, pitching seas.

A Nexian fights with the sheer power of the mind alone, amplified tens of thousands of times over by the weird science magic of his helm, a mental focusing and projecting device of uncanny power. Before the telepathic attack, any ordinary man is utterly helpless to defend himself or fight back, unless he is equipped with a comparable device. The attack is one of externally induced illusion. That first blow to Thane's belly had felt like an invisible hammer: actually, the Nexian had projected a telepathic bolt directly to those nerve centers of Thane's mind connected to the stomach, *simulating* the neural patterns such a blow would cause. The brain could not tell the difference between the neural simulation and the real thing: it simply registered *pain!*

Exhausted, limp from the mental pumeling, Thane sprawled on the deck. Invisible whip blows lashed across his back, stinging as if he were being flayed with nettles. He flopped and kicked like a beached fish . . . and beneath the mind-induced torment, he felt cold tendrils insinuate between the fibers of his brain! Behind the howling thunder of the physical torment, the Nexian was probing along his neuronic linkages, rifling through his stored memories!

It was a debasing experience. Rape of the mind is the ultimate degradation, and—despite his bodily agony—something, some inner core of untapped strength within Thane—*rebelled!* Fought back!

Now the icy tendrils were fumbling within the deepest centers of the mind . . . crudely, roughly tearing through delicate webwork of woven thought, as a barbarian tomb-robber smashes his way through

precious artworks, seeking hidden gold. Thane felt
something spark to life deep within himself . . . raw
fury coiled like a tightening spring . . . intolerable
pressure was building up, deep within the very core of
his being, struggling like a chained Titan for furious
release . . . *something had to give—*

There was a click within his head. Some invisible
barrier in his brain cracked, gave way before a surge
of force that flooded suddenly through every nerve
and muscle of his body . . . a glowing, tingling, electric flood of new energy from some unknown brain
center. It was as if, in the utter extremity of his need,
Thane had tapped some hidden source of unknown
power.

Strength surged through his rippling muscles, seizing mastery over his nerves, deadening the artificially
induced stimuli of pain, lending uncanny resources to
his whipped and beaten body. He sprang erect, eyes
blazing with naked fury. Zangor paused, jaws sagging
with shock, seeing the fallen, conquered foe revive.
Laughter stilled, as if a sound track had been
abruptly turned off. Silence fell.

Thane strained his magnificent body and mind in
some mysterious new way, like flexing a muscle you
never knew you possessed before. Tension coiled
within his alert, clear mind which no longer was
clouded with crimson pain.

He drove a mental bolt at Zangor's brain.

He had no idea how he did it. But, then, neither
could he precisely describe how he could hurl a fist at
an opponent: a thousand nerves activated a complex
web of muscles in just such a manner as to lift and
move the limb . . . but the process is instinctive and

instantaneous. So was it with his newly won mental weapon.

Zangor screamed as the bolt of mental force smashed against his mind with brain-numbing impact. He staggered, shaken as Thane drove him back step by step with a ringing series of smashing blows.

It was weirdly exhilarating for the warrior of Zha. There was a curious new thrill in using your mind in this strange new way, like a new limb you have never activated till now. Thane experimented with his new discovery. He had heard of rare individuals gifted with unusual psionic talents such as psycho-kinesis . . . he *lifted* . . .

Zangor floated up from the deck like some ungainly balloon, wallowing and rolling helplessly in mid-air, limbs flopping and kicking helplessly. Then Thane cut off the power and the Mind Gladiator fell, smashing flat against the deck plates. He lay limp as a dead thing, his head lolling, eyes glazed and open, staring.

Then, as swiftly as it had awakened within him, Thane's weird mental power deserted him. It was as abrupt as if an unseen hand had reached out and turned off an electric switch. Strength drained from his magnificent body: his limbs sagged under a crushing burden of fatigue. His head swam drunkenly, mind blurring, sight failing in a crimson fog.

He did not even know that he was falling until he felt the steel on his face.

After that, he knew nothing at all . . .

7 JUNGLE MOON

It was like being imprisoned within a dream. He swam slowly upward through coiling opalescent mists that flushed through shades of chartreuse and amber, melting rose and purest flame until he was bathed at last in utter white light. For all the sense of vision, he could feel nothing, his body gave no sense impressions for the nerves to transport to the brain. Dimly, as in a waking dream, he was aware of being lifted by rough hands and dragged from the arena . . . he saw, as if through clouds of swirling colored fog, faces peering down at him, faces curious, hating, envious, fearful.

He was dumped into his cell and loaded with manacles and chains, but his mind was somehow insulated from the senses of his body, as if the million nerve endings of the flesh were wrapped in cotton. He could not feel the cold deck plates beneath his naked back, nor the chill constriction of the chains, nor even the hypospray when it was pressed against the base of his throat by the young shaman in the green robes. Yet he was intricately aware of the drug which seethed through his branching veins from the injection . . . he could almost trace its invisible and multiple path as it wove through his body and spread its deadly fog through his brain.

Then sight itself went away and left him in the embrace of utter darkness.

Obviously, Shastar feared his peculiar powers—but did not dare to kill him. Shastar *wanted* something from him, something so precious that the bandit chieftain was even willing to permit him to live within the very stronghold of his power, although a wiser man would have feared the curious mental force that Thane had unexpectedly demonstrated in the arena.

Strange . . . strange!

The drug, a subtle narcotic from far Delaquoth the Drug Blenders' Planet, anesthetized his body but in some curious mode, it simultaneously stimulated his mind. It attained crystal clarity; new linkages fell into connection between brain synapses; his mind became capable of super logic. It was as if as recompense for loss of bodily senses, his mental vision was doubled.

He was now "aware" of his body in a manner hitherto unknown. Like staring at an intricate map, the tangled system of blood veins and arteries, the nerve system and neural paths were laid out before him. His new mind explored his recumbent body cell by cell, like an eye scanning a chart or sensitive fingers tracing a raised pattern.

Was this the action of the drug? No—surely, Shastar could not intend to increase his captive's mental resources! It must be a new development of the weird mind powers that had risen within him under the psychic punishment he had experienced from Zangor the Mind Gladiator.

He extended his mental sensors beyond his body.

Swift as light, these intangible extensions of his mind flashed through the ship—and beyond, to the black abyss of space itself.

He watched as the giant warship emerged from the Interplenum into normal vacuum, braking as it approached its home port. Ahead of them, the Red Moon grew, a swollen, sanguine orb bathed in bloody light from its aging primary. It looked like a vast round shield, heated red-hot in the fires of some cosmic hell . . . or the glowering angry eye of some stellar Cyclops, glaring at their approach.

The ship braked, dropped, hovered and floated over the swollen orb. In some remote era of Imperial technology, the satellite had been terraformed: its core hollowed out and fitted with gravity engines, an artificial atmosphere supplied, and the rugged rocky surface layered with topsoil and seeded with vegetation.

For it was a jungle moon, this lone companion to the lost planet, Phiolanthe. Weird under its red radiance, odd vegetation clothed its peaks and hills. Enormous toadstools nodded atop slim stalks, bowing in the perfumed breeze. A fungoid forest filled with domed and hooded growths, spotted, banded, flecked and auraed, bloomed like nightmarish flowers about still pools of fluid that looked like lakes of blood beneath the red sky of flame.

A cluster of needle peaks whipped into view over the near horizon. Thane's eerie mental vision saw a fantastic castle of black stone, hewn from the spires of a sheer cliff, that lifted jagged crenelations against the sky of crimson vapor. The Red Moon banner whipped from tower top and dome. Steel-clad guards leaned on barbaric spears at stations along the walls.

They had arrived at the mountain citadel of Shastar.

Thane's control of his mind powers grew with experience. He was newly aware of overlapping levels
of Time, like many sheets of transparent paper
through which temporal intervals could be observed
in progression. He was simultaneously aware of the
ship hanging in space—of its landing—of the bandits
disgorging from the hold, bearing his unconscious
body and Illara in chains—and of their being locked
in cells high up in the black towers of the mountain
top fortress.

It was all like actions glimpsed in a dream, devoid
of urgency or of sensory immediacy.

With his new power of logical deduction he could
scan a series of isolated facts and connect them into a
pattern. He knew now that his attempted escape had
been falling in with Shastar's plan. The bandit chief
had planned to engineer some overtly hostile act on
Thane's part, to lure or provoke him into revolt,
whereupon he would have a good reason to hurl him
into the arena and pit him against Zangor the Mind
Gladiator.

There Shastar had shrewdly planned for the Gladiator to pummel him unmercifully. Starworld legends
whispered that the Nexian-trained Mentalists could
probe a mind, once its natural barriers had been broken down by pain. After subjecting Thane to crushing
mental punishment to the point that his inborn mind
defenses crumbled, Zangor had then been instructed
to explore Thane's broken mind, extracting therefrom
the secrets for which Shastar had hunted down and
captured the warrior.

This secret could only be the hiding place of the

Jewel of Amzar, the sacred talisman of the Time Priests.

The conclusion was inescapable: *the chieftain was after the Time Tower—the fabled treasure trove of the Aealim!*

And . . . what of Prince Chan? Was he too seeking the lost Jewel that was reputed to be the magic key to the Time Treasure of the Children of the Fire Mist?

Were Chan and Shastar rivals? Thane brooded, bringing the enormous mental clarity of his newly strengthened brain to bear upon the complex tangle of actions and motives.

And whence had come this strange mental power? Had his mind reacted under the mind torture, by awakening a dormant talent inherent to each man? Or was this another manifestation of Thane's weird powers . . . the powers he had so strangely won years ago?

For years now, the Swordsman of Zha had possessed an erratic and uncontrollable mind talent to bridge time itself. The power came and went, was impossible to summon and difficult to hold in focus. By this power, back in the tavern on Daikoon, he had "seen" Prince Chan behind the booth curtain, had foreknown of the bully's intent. Hence he had drawn surreptitiously his pistol and scarfed it from view, awaiting the Chadorian's crude attempt to pick a quarrel.

The same talent, or one like it, had empowered him to read the dwarfed enchanter's secret past. By a sort of psychometry he had "read" Druu's history and been able to shake the little hunchback with a revelation of his secrets. The same time-lapsing skill en-

abled him to counter the dwarf's sigil with the coun-
tersign he had traced in wine upon the table top. This
same uncanny foreknowledge of the future and re-
trospective vision into the past had aided him to escape from many traps over his adventurous years' of
thievery and banditry and roving.

Now these powers had come under his conscious
control, together with amazing new mind skills
. . . for what purpose?

However they had come to him, Thane knew the
time had come to *use* his new found powers. He determined to escape from the Red Moon with Illara,
and he knew with a triumphant surge of exaltation
that no force of magic or science could any longer
stand in his way. *The powers of a God were his—and
now he must use them!*

He awoke. He rose, the shackles falling from him
like strands of broken silk. Exerting mastery over
body and mind, he shrugged off the sense-deadening
powers of the Delaquothyan drug. Full clarity of
mind was his. His body was alert, refreshed, limber as
that of a superb athlete.

Thane stood in a cell high up in the tower of Shastar's clifftop eyrie. The walls of solid stone were
sheathed in tough steel. The door was a slab of steel,
inches thick, windowless. Using his sensories, Thane
probed through the massive door as if it were a pane
of glass. In the hall beyond a squad of soldiers
guarded egress. They were heavily armored in suits
of impenetrable black mail, with visored helms, and
they bore gas tubes and dart-throwers whose needle
projectiles were dipped in the Red Lotus, a potent
paralysis drug.

With his new super powers, Thane might be able to win through their ranks to the stairs beyond, but doubtless they could spread the alarm and rouse the entire strength of the black castle against him. Secrecy and swiftness were the best tools for his escape.

He turned to the window. It was heavily barred with a massive grill of steel rods two inches thick. Only chinks of red sky could peek through the narrow interstices.

Thane directed the force of his amazing brain against this barrier—

He reached into the molecular level of the steel, twisting the structure of molecules into new alignments, using projected fields of mind magnetism as his tools. The crystal structure of the steel altered . . . shifted into new lattice formations . . . and the solid steel bars became as fragile as rods of thin glass. For a long moment the prison cell thrummed and quivered as strange cosmic forces played throughout it—stupendous forces, such as those unimaginable electromagnetic fields that thunder in the fiery core of mighty stars, or seethe and vibrate in the uppermost atmospheric levels of heavy gravity planets . . . the very air and light within the room was torn and dimmed, shaken by ultimate energies. Then all was still.

Thane reached up and tore the grill from the window in one piece.

In his strong hands, the steel bars snapped and broke like tubes of thin glass. He laid the broken grill on the floor and sprang lithely into the open window.

It was cut deep out of the solid stone of the castle wall, which was a foot thick and more. Crouching in the newly-made opening, he looked out at the wild red jungles of the moonscape. He looked down . . .

and the cliff fell sheerly away beneath him, dropping to the distant glimmer of a red moat far below. He looked up and saw a slim thunderhawk of a space-boat hovering above the castle, tethered to the topmost spire with a mooring line, floating weightless on its anti-gravity fields.

His unlimited mind reached out through the strange dimensions of mental force, searching the castle for Illara. He rifled through mind after mind, as a clerk searched swiftly through a stack of file cards, not pausing to note the full contents of each, but watching for key symbols.

Then he found her. She was in a room like his, further down the castle wall. She too was alone and locked in.

He stared out at the red jungles, now brooding in a heavy scarlet twilight as the black bulk of the dead world of Phiolanthe had swung between the Red Moon and the dying star. He thought . . . in the arena, he had lifted Zangor's body by sheer force of mind alone . . . could he now levitate his own? In the unguessable regions of his mind, he searched for the key—*and found it.*

Reaching with intangible fields of force, he took hold of the moon's magnetic field, and floated out of the window into the dim twilight air like some weird golden bird, his crimson mane floating behind him like weightless coils of smoke on heavy air.

He drifted along the castle wall, concentrating on keeping his body aloft. He discovered how to move, and let his mind charge his body with positive magnetic fields while he reached out and formed a negative field in the air before him. This way, he propelled himself forward through the murky air.

It was an eerie eperience, like flying in a dream, but he discovered it took utmost concentration, for once, when he allowed his mind to drift into other patterns of thinking, he wavered and fell, dropping like a stone as his hold on the magnetic fields slackened through inattention. Thereafter, he kept his mind directed on the purpose at hand.

He came to the window of the cell, and hovered beyond it, clinging with one hand to the barred grill. Peering in, he could just make out the white form of Illara by the dim illumination. She seemed to be weeping.

He called her name softly, and she came to the window, her white face incredulous, the jewel in her ear flashing weirdly in the dim red radiance.

"Thane! How did you—?" She gasped in amazement. He silenced her swiftly.

"Don't arouse the whole castle, girl! Hush—and stand back from in front of the window, I'm going to get you out of there—*hurry, now,* do as I say and get out of the way!"

Her face vanished from the grill, and Thane hovered there thinking for a moment. He wondered if he could keep himself weightless while simultaneously realigning the crystalline lattice structure of the steel bars, as he had done to effect his own escape. He decided that he probably could not. And, anyway, he sensed that his mind was rapidly tiring with all this unusual mental exercise. He must get her out—and quickly—before he exhausted his new mental powers.

He pictured what would happen to him, hovering here hundreds of yards above that crimson moat, if his power of self-levitation failed suddenly. The thought dewed his brow with cold perspiration.

Gathering his mind powers into focus, he projected a powerful ray of force at the steel bars.

They melted into a glittering vapor of steel particles.

The action had taken but an instant of his attention, yet in that instant, he fell through the dim murky light, and only with difficulty did he regain his hold on the moon's magnetic field, slowly lifting himself again to the level of the window.

Impatiently, he called Illara to the window and told her to clasp her arms about his neck. Wordlessly, she did so, and he drew her out of the opening in the wall, supporting her added weight with an extra surge of mental stamina.

"How—*how*—?" she stammered, awed at his incredible magic powers.

"No time for talk! My power is fading rapidly," he mumbled. "Hold on . . ."

He lifted again, and they floated up past the rough wall of black stone. Up . . . up . . . up, till he thought his brain would crumble at the sheer effort of levitating their double weight . . .

He could feel the warmth of her white arms clasped about his corded neck, and the warm perfume of her hair in his gasping nostrils. His senses swam, dizzy with vertigo. The strength was draining from his mind with every yard. It seemed to take ever greater effort to lift ever higher, as if the higher they went, the amount of mental energies needed increased by mathematical progression.

At any moment, he knew, his newborn faculties might fail, hurtling them to a terrible death on the rocky shore of the moat far below. He clung to consciousness with a terrible urgency, fighting for every breath, fighting for every yard of space, and the circle of his awareness shrank to the narrow circumference of their two bodies which clung desperately together in thin air, a thousand feet above the crimson waters of the ghostly lake.

Then his strength failed and his mind went black—

8 THE VOICE FROM THE OPAL

HE HAD BEEN CLINGING to the edge of a cliff for a hundred years. A tremendous weight was dragging him down to crimson death, like an iron hand clamped about his body and pulling him down with crushing force.

A screaming bird beat and cried in his ears, but he could scarcely hear its shrieking cry for the thunder of surf in his ears.

His head was splitting under hammer blows of intolerable agony. It was like an iron bell being beaten upon a red hot anvil.

It would be so easy to let go, so easy to stop fighting, there would be a swift drop into darkness . . . and then all would end and he could sleep at last, could . . . rest . . .

The screaming bird was louder now.

It was calling his name.

"Thane!—*Thane!*"

He shook his head numbly, like an injured thing. All he wanted to do was to relax his grip . . . to let go . . . to fall into the endless darkness . . . to . . . *sleep* . . .

"Thane! *Help me!*"

He came to his senses all at once: waking to full, tingling consciousness.

He was clinging to the steel rim of an entry-port by his fingers. The slim weight of Illara about his neck was an iron weight dragging him down. His dangling heels kicked and found only emptyness.

With a sudden flash of mental clarity he knew what had happened. Shaking his head to clear his mind of the roaring scarlet mists, he thought furiously. Just as they had floated up to the belly of the moored ship, his newfound powers of levitation had failed—*just as he reached up and took hold of the edge of the port in the belly hold!*

Icy perspiration drenched his body. He must have continued to cling to the edge of the airlock door by sheer tenacity of will alone, although his mind had completely blacked out! It was a terrifying thought . . . he had been unconscious, and nothing but the in-born instinct of self-preservation had kept his fingers clamped on that cold steel lip that was biting into his flesh.

Now, summoning his last reserves of strength, he levered himself up and into the open port, the extra weight of the girl who still clung about his neck seeming like an intolerable added hardship.

His muscles strained and creaked with the effort. Needles of hot pain drove through his skull. It felt like his arms were being torn slowly out of their sockets. But, somehow, he hauled himself up and through the yawning hole, and sprawled gasping in the hold of the little spaceboat.

Illara rolled away from him, and sat up hugging her white knees and gave vent to a fit of trembling.

He simply lay for a time without moving, drinking in the clear, cold air like a thirsty man gulping iced wine, feeling relief roll through his aching body in great warm waves. It had been a close thing. Closer than he liked to think about . . .

After a while he dragged himself to his feet and stood. He went over to the huddled, sobbing girl and drew her up into the circle of his arms and kissed her tears away. She clung to him warmly, slowly quieting.

Then they began to explore the ship. Thank Onolk, the Spacegod, it was empty!

"This must be a patrol boat," he said thoughtfully, "or one of Shastar's courier gigs."

"What are we going to do?"

He gave her a grin. "Escape in it! Come on—there's no time to lose. At any moment one of Shastar's goons may peek in to find the cells empty."

They went forward to the control cabin and strapped themselves in the two pilot chairs. Thane ran a practiced hand over the knobs, triggering the drive into action. He thumbed switches, closing and sealing the entry port, dropping the mooring line, raising the antigravity field into a higher octave of power.

The trim little craft lifted up from the frowning walls of Shastar's keep and went whistling through the upper atmosphere of the Red Moon, hurtling like a fleet hawk above the red fungus forests and glittering lakes of liquid fire. Within moments they had skimmed out of the moon's envelope of air and rocketed into space. With Thane's hands on the controls, they swung in a wide orbit around the dark bulk of the dead world of Phiolanthe until the planet's mass hid them from any electronic surveillance of the Red

Moon. Then the spaceboat angled off sharply into interstellar space. The dim red spark of the dying star shrank behind them.

"Where are we going?" Illara asked, as Thane locked the control consoles, engaged the robot pilot, and unbuckled himself from the chair.

"Nowhere. Anywhere," he shrugged. He went back into the small galley and found it well stocked. He came back into the cabin with a flask of smoky yellow wine tucked under his arm and his hands filled with cheese, black bread, cold beef and fruit. The drain on his mental and physical powers left him aching with hunger.

"We can't translate into Interplenum yet, because that broadcasts an aura of radionic energy which would show up on Shastar's scopes," he mumbled around a mouthful of utterly delicious spiced meat. He washed the mouthful down with a cold draught of tingling wine and wiped his mouth on the back of his hand. He offered food to the girl and helped her out of the chair. They sprawled out on an acceleration couch and wolfed down the meal.

"You know the entropy levels of normal and of Interplenal space are very different," he explained, "and that shifting from one to the other releases a compensatory burst of *omega* particles. Well, let's not give our recent host any clue to the direction we have taken. We'll go out a few light minutes first, so to be out of range of his scopes. Then I'll take you back to Daikoon, or wherever you want to go . . ."

Thane slept deeply and dreamlessly, his exhausted tissues drinking in strength during rest as a parched sponge absorbs moisture.

They woke, and ate again. By now it was safe to translate the trim little spaceboat into Interplenum, and Thane did so. Within an hour or so, they would arrive at decelleration point for a landing on Daikoon the Desert World.

"Thane, what did you do . . . how did you overcome the Mind Gladiator in the ship arena? And disintegrate the bars in my cell and *fly?*" she asked. They were lying at ease on the couch, her small head pillowed on his brawny arm.

The warrior kissed her lightly, considering how to explain something which he himself did not fully understand.

"Seven years ago," he began slowly, "I was with a gang of star pirates. We made a raid on Mnom the Dark World, knowing the Time Priests who dwell on that shadowy planet are without armies or defenses, and have amassed a trove of golden treasure sent as offerings to their shrines by the Planet Princes of half the Near Stars."

"Yes . . . go on."

He shrugged. "There's not much to tell. We took the City of the Time Temple without bloodshed—a mere show of force did the trick. We landed and started to loot the shrines. I was in the vanguard. At the inner shrine, I saw an enormous gem on top of a great altar of black marble, and took it for my prize." His brow wrinkled with memory. "Huge it was, and strange . . . a great cloudly ball of rough crystal, split into ten thousand glittering facets and prisms, and filled with misty light, like coiled fires . . . I was staring into it, trying to estimate its worth, when one of the priests broke free of my men, who were holding them at laser point. He ran up to me, screaming something about 'the sacred talisman' and 'sacrilege against the Time Wizards of Aea' . . . and he seized my arm. I dropped the crystal, and it broke, there on the marble steps of the altar: shattered into a million ringing shards of glittering dust . . ."

Brooding, he stared through the cabin wall as if peering into the mists of the past. The girl beside him whispered a query, and his reverie broke.

"I was looking down at the broken jewel when I saw something . . . a mist . . . a glittering smoke . . . a cloud of radiant diamond dust or star sparkles . . . rising from the crystal wreckage. I don't know what it was. I don't know whether the jewel was hollow and contained the fog of light, or whether it was solid and the radiance was stored within the crystal structure, like electricity within a battery. I only know that it was there, and that the smashing of the gem released it."

He rubbed his jaw and combed a nervous hand through his scarlet mane.

"And then it . . . *entered into me*," he said tightly. And, seeing the girl's startled eyes widen, he laughed harshly. "Oh, it didn't burn! There was no pain. No sensation at all . . . I just stood there like a stupid moon ox, watching the swirling tendrils of glowing mist seep into my body . . . it soaked into my flesh and was gone. Nothing happened . . . nothing at all: there was a sort of electric tingle that ran throughout me, a shivery feeling that set my flesh crawling, a coldness at the base of my brain . . . but these went away, and nothing happened. I shrugged it off as some curious freak accident. *Then I passed out cold!*"

He grinned at the memory.

"The next thing I knew, I was lying on a pallet in

the innermost shrine—the 'holy of holies' and being treated as if I were an incarnate God. The pirates had looted and left, thinking I had been struck down by divine vengeance. There I was, waited on hand and foot by priests who treated me with such reverence as to my slightest wishes that I felt like an Emperor.

"Well, we got along all right. The old priest who had joggled my arm—his name was Chastrophar— tended me. I was weak as a kitten and the very slightest movement or exertion left me totally exhausted. Oh, he explained what it was—I had received some sort of electrostatic charge from the Jewel of Amzar (that's what the Time Priests called the crystal I had broken). The shock overloaded my nerve system and nearly burned out my brain—you know, of course, that nerves conduct stimuli to the brain just as wire conducts electricity, and that thought and feeling are essentially just electrical impulses.

"Well, it took me seven months to get on my feet again. I had to sort of relearn to use my body all over again. And I got a series of mind exercises of a sort, learned a form of mental discipline that began to do strange things to me. I discovered that I could see into the past by a sort of psychometry . . . and look ahead into the future by a sort of prescience, not much, just ten minutes or a half hour ahead, but a little. It was weird. I asked old Chastrophar why this was so, and why I was treated with such reverence, and he explained it to me. Oh, it made quite a tale!

"It seems the Time Priests of Mnom worship a race of gods known throughout the Near Stars by various terms—the Children of Aea, the Time Wizards, the Aealim, the Children of the Fire Mist, and so on. But they weren't real gods, just a race of beings who had come into the galaxy a billion years before the advent of Man, then left for some unknown region beyond the Universe called 'The Fire Mist.' They were not human—they weren't even made of flesh and blood. They were creatures of pure thought, pure patterns of energy, clouds of electrons. And they could pass through time as easily as we pass through space. Not being creatures of matter they were not bound to space alone, but could travel to the past or the future. And when they left the galaxy, one of them remained behind, frozen in what Chastrophar called 'a stasis crystal'—sleeping or dead, I don't know. They were immortal, you see: like energy, *being* nothing but energy, they could neither be created nor destroyed. And when I broke the stasis crystal, the Jewel of Amzar, the Immortal within it entered my body . . . or enough of it entered, to give me a sort of halfway vision into the future and a small distance into the past.

"*That* was why the priests handled me with such reverence—*I had a God dwelling within me!*"

"And . . . what happened finally, Thane?" she asked, wonder and awe and something else—dread?—in her voice. "How did you come to leave Mnom?"

"When I was fit and hardy again, one of the Planet Princes came with his retinue to worship and make sacrifice before the Time Temple. I joined his guard, passing myself off as a wandering mercenary. I never went back to the Dark World again. It's hard enough to be a *man;* playing the role of a God is too much to ask!"

She stared up at him through the dusk of the

dimly-lit cabin. Her violet eyes were enormous, shadowed by some strange film of emotion.

"And . . . what happened in the arena?"

"When the Mind Gladiator began knocking my brain loose, he may have joggled some connections loose—awakened some dormant telepathic talent already supercharged by my exposure to that dead Child of the Fire Mist whose time-traveling energies had entered my body. I guess it was something like that. I found I could project rays and probes of mental force; could levitate others, as well as myself . . . could change the molecular structure of steel bars by mere thought alone . . ."

"But . . . if the Time Crystal is destroyed . . . why didn't you *tell* Shastar? He might have let us go!"

"Sure. He *might* have. But he *might* have disposed of us down the nearest disintegrator chute, as superfluous cargo. Besides," he grinned, "I'm an ornery cuss. I don't like being pushed around, being forced to do things."

At that moment a cold mocking voice filled the spaceboat cabin.

"I think we've heard enough, Illara. We know all the facts. I think you can immobilize him now!"

Like a leaping tiger, Thane was off the couch in a bound and crouched naked in the center of the cabin, searching with supersenses for the source of the metallic voice.

It had come from the huge moony opal clipped to the girl's earlobe!

He swing toward her with hot questions on his lips, but a shade too slowly . . . the paralysis gun in her slim white fingers speared him with a ray of purple light the same hue as her great sad eyes and he fell forward, his mind a well of roaring blackness.

The last thing he saw was those eyes, enormous, misty purple, filled with great tears. Then the lights went out.

9 SLAVES OF CHAN

"He's coming out of it now, Master," the voice said.

Thane became fully awake, his senses returning on the instant, without the usual hazy transition phase. He lay still, however, eyes closed. His ears registered the dull throb of spacecraft engines; his sense of touch told him he was sprawled on an acceleration couch strewn with choicest furs. The voice had been one that he remembered hearing before . . . then it came back to him. That shrill, whining voice. *Druu, the dwarfed enchanter from Yoth Zembis who had sought to buy his services for Prince Chan back in the inn at Zotheera!*

He reached out with his mind, extending a sensor . . . but with tendril *faded*. He attempted to scan the cabin again, but found his mental powers strangely inoperative.

There was nothing else to do, so he opened his eyes.

Chan's face, coldly handsome, mocking and sardonic, smiled down at him. His eyes were filled with icy amusement, like chips of frozen rubies . . . as cold and hard and deadly as the black snout of the laser pistol he held, directed straight at the swordsman's heart.

"So you are back with us again, eh? And how do you feel?" the Prince asked in a smooth voice.

"Better than you look," Thane grunted. He rose up on one elbow and peered around through the half light. He was in a spaceship cabin, richly furnished and lavish with ornament and decoration. Soft lights glimmered along walls paneled with mellow harpwood from Vega VI; tapestries woven of fabulous crystal cloth by the sentient Arachnidae of Algol shimmered like iridescent mist; the air was heavy with perfumed smoke which coiled in blue whorls and spirals from a brazier of pierced silver in the corner.

The ugly little dwarf stood at the further end of the couch manipulating an instrument. Thane could not make out its shape—his eyes were blurred and his brain ached dully. He was vaguely surprised to find he was not bound. He swung his bare legs over the edge of the fur strewn couch and sat up, peering about him through the haze of incense.

"I could use some wine," he muttered.

"Druu, bring him a drink."

He gulped down a goblet of that fiery purple liquor the Eophim vintners distill from their wine apples and felt the ache within his brain subside. *The girl had betrayed him, that was clear . . . she was an agent of Prince Chan all the time . . . everything about her was a lie . . .*

With a feeling of inward emptiness, he wondered if she had been lying back in the cave on Daikoon. But there was no time for thought now: Chan was speaking in his smooth, cold voice.

"With the 'dampener' switched on, your mental powers cannot function; I am sorry if this causes your head to ache, but I must take every precaution to protect myself against coming to the same end as Zangor." The Prince allowed himself a chill little smile.

"Dampener?" Thane asked.

The Prince waved the snout of his pistol toward the instrument that Druu was tending. It was a tangle of steel and glass tubes and glowing red sparks of light.

"They learn the science wisdom of the Ancients, these sorcerors of Yoth Zembis, as well as the Dark Lore of sigil and cantrip," the albino observed. "This instrument broadcasts a fluctuating electromagnetic current aligned to the frequencies of human thought. It has an inhibiting effect on the nerve centers of the brain, cutting down mental activity. Rather on the same principle as using one radio set to 'jam' the waves emanating from another."

"Clever," Thane said sourly, tossing down the last of the brandy.

"You have yet to discover just how clever I have been about this whole business," the Prince smiled.

"Yes, I suppose you have been," Thane said. "Like planting the girl on me, with a miniature transceiver inside that hollowed gem. That *was* clever!"

Chan's ruby eyes narrowed to glittering slits. His voice purred with oily amusement.

"Yes, a woman makes a fine weapon in capable hands . . . slim and supple as a sword blade . . . and a blade to which no man's armor is completely proof. Defend himself how he will, a woman's sharp wits and pointed tongue can find the chink in his armor . . . as Illara found the chink in yours. I think she cut her way into your heart, eh?"

Thane pretended to laugh, but it rang hollow in his ears, and he didn't think it fooled Prince Chan.

"Into my heart! Gods, no. She means nothing to me . . . just an amiable bit of girl flesh to while away an idle hour or two with."

Chan smiled. "Perhaps. But it did not sound that way from the other end of the broadcasting beam . . ." Noting Thane's flush, he chuckled softly. "However, it is of no matter; the girl has served her purpose and brought me the information Shastar and I needed before we could progress further with our plans."

Thane felt his temper rising; he controlled himself with effort.

"So the chieftain is in this thing, too, eh? I suspected as much! And the matter of the seven gold dragons—that was just a blind? And the band of Desert Warriors chasing the girl, back on Daikoon—that was a blind, too . . ."

"That is correct. Shastar and I are together in this, partners with equal shares in the treasure . . ."

"Treasure?" Thane inquired lazily.

Chan sat back in a great thronelike chair of Netharnan silverwood. "Yes . . . let me tell you a tale, swordsman. Aeons ago, the Children of the Fire Mist ruled this galaxy. When they left, they left behind a stupendous trove of treasure they had looted from a million ages of time—the loot of a thousand worlds and eras, the wealth of empires yet unborn, plucked from the treasure cities of many worlds by these pirates of the time trails. This treasure they sealed within an impenetrable tower on an unknown planet

far in the future . . . billions of years hence, when
life has died on every world in the universe, and
nothing is left but a handful of fading suns ebbing toward extinction . . . dying like burning coals, in the
last days of this galaxy when the few remaining suns
spin through a dark and empty void poised on the
very brink of Eternity. This Tower Beyond Time is
whispered in ancient legend and elder lore on a thousand worlds, and no man can ever reach it, for it lies
distant from us in *time*, not in space, and no one
can travel the time trails save for the Aealim
themselves . . . and there we stayed, Shastar and I,
both of us apart and seeking the Time Treasure, with
no hope of ever attaining to it. For who can move
through time, save for the Aealim alone? And then we
heard of you."

"And what of me?"

"We heard that a star pirate had seized the Jewel
of Amzar from the high altar of Mnom. And we
heard, as well, that this crystal talisman was left behind by the Children of Aea, and that it contains a
certain kind of power . . . the key to the Web . . . the
key that would unlock the Tower."

"I see . . ."

"And so we searched for you, Shastar and I, and in
our dual quest we became aware of each other. At
first, we fought, but soon we realized the futility of
this. Surely the Tower contained treasure enough for
two! So we joined forces to hunt you down, wherever
you may have wandered in all those years since you
left the Dark World. We had but your description,
and the crimson hair suggested a warrior from Zha
the Jungle Planet . . . and the characteristic use of

two scimitars when you fought. And at last we found you."

"So you did, but had no joy of it," Thane grinned.

Chan was not amused; he shot the Zhayan a cold glance and the pistol never wavered from Thane's heart.

"I sent my Chadorian bravo in, to test you, to see what kind of a man you were and to see how you fought. And through my enchanter I sought to purchase your services. Both attempts were a failure. Then I permitted you to escape, and laid a trap for you, baited with the girl. We planned, Shastar and I, to seize you and take the gem from you by force. If that failed, and you did not have the jewel, Shastar was to use his Mind Gadiator to search your brain for the hiding place of the talisman. If all else failed, we thought to use the girl to wheedle from you information about the Jewel . . ."

"She did her job well," Thane said coldly. "I hope she is well paid for her trouble."

"The girl is a slave, and does not work for pay, but to avoid the lash," Chan said coolly, and Thane decided at that moment that he would kill the albino princeling before this adventure ended. He thought of Illara's slender beauty, her wide fawnlike eyes and soft mouth and slim warm white body, with the cruel lash of a whip curling about it, and he decided he would crush the life from Chan's throat with his naked hands when all this was over.

"We did not count on your uncanny mind powers," the Prince admitted. "Of those we knew nothing, thus all our attempts failed—you crippled my Chadorian and slew the Mind Gadiator and escaped from Shastar's impregnable moon fort—but the girl played her part well, and got you to talk, and over the radio beam, I heard everything."

"And now?"

Chan shrugged easily. "I tried to buy your services. Now I will have them at gunpoint, if there is no other way. But I would prefer that you joined us of your own free will."

Thane regarded him warily.

"As another—partner?"

Chan's expression was guileless, his voice smooth and bland.

"Why not? The Tower hoards wealth beyond calculation—the loot of a galaxy. There is enough for—three."

Thane was incredulous, but tried not to show it.

"You mean you want me to join you in this venture, for a third of the treasure trove?" he demanded. The Prince nodded calmly.

"There is enough—and more—for all concerned. We shall, the three of us, be wealthy beyond the dreams of emperors," he said. But Thane had no illusions: once he had done his part and opened the treasure tower, his payment would be on the tip of a knife, or the trigger of a laser gun. He pretended, however, to fall in with Chan's scheme.

"That sounds fair to me, aye, more than fair! But—aren't you forgetting one thing?" he countered. The Prince regarded him curiously.

"What have I overlooked?"

"The Jewel of Amzar," Thane said, "is broken. Smashed to a thousand fragments. Whatever key or power it once held must have dissipated when it broke."

Chan was unruffled at this, his voice serene.

"Perhaps. Or perhaps not. You told Illara that when the crystal talisman broke, a 'fog of light' entered your body, and that the Time Priests of Mnom tended you with awe and reverence, as if your flesh housed an incarnate God. Well, I know nothing of Gods, incarnate or not—but your body *may* hold the key to the Web. At any rate, we shall see. But what of my offer, warrior?"

Thane shrugged.

"Why not? If I do not cooperate with you willingly, you will force me at the point of a gun. And if you will promise to reward my cooperation with one third of the hoard . . . what have I to lose?"

Chan was pleased.

"I am glad that you see things in that light, and bear no grudges for what we were forced to do. Very well, then, we are agreed." And, with that, he rose, and put away the gun. "The dampener, however, will stay on. For a while, anyway. Otherwise, you might decide to use your mental magic and go and seek the treasure all on your own. It is safer this way . . ."

Thane shrugged.

"As you please . . ."

They gave him a cabin in the rear of Chan's spacious and luxurious yacht. Illara he did not see, nor did he really want to: the memory of her betrayal rankled deep within him, although he cursed himself for feeling so deeply over a mere woman. It rankled, in fact, deeper than he himself really knew. Had he begun to fall in love with her, there in that cave in the moonlit deserts of Daikoon? He told himself it was impossible, she was a slut, a plaything of Chan's, a tool in his hand, nothing more.

But he did not succeed in convincing himself.

They slept and ate and slept again.

When Illara had caught him offguard with the paralysis gun and stunned him into unconsciousness, Chan had bade her halt the ship. He had boarded the stolen spaceboat and taken the girl and Thane aboard his own craft, which had been following the broadcast beam of Illara's hidden transceiver, unknown to Thane. Now they must retrace the path of Thane's flight and take aboard Shastar and a crew of his hardy warriors. Then they would fly directly to the Dark World and try to see if Thane could activate the Web of the Aealim.

This Web was some sort of an interdimensional gateway or fixed transit point in time. The Children of the Fire Mist had built it billions of years ago, and left it on Mnom to be guarded by the Time Priests.

Could Thane with all his Aealim time powers— open it?

And if he did—what? He had no illusions as to the veracity of Chan's partnership offer. He knew that the moment the Prince's need of him was ended—his life would be ended. If it were not for that brain-inhibiting mechanism of Druu's, Thane could break free of these entanglements . . . perhaps, even without his mind powers, he could overcome the Prince and . . . but no. He decided to see this adventure through to the finish.

The one thing that did not occur to Thane was— what would happen if his mental powers did indeed hold the key? What would happen if he managed to penetrate the Web, and they ventured through the unborn ages of the future, to reach the strange fortress built on the very edge of Eternity by that strange and shadowy God race who had so mysteriously left their mark on the future of the galaxy?

What would they find, there on the farthest shore of infinite time, on the brink of the Unknown, in that distant age when the entire Universe tottered on the knife sharp brink of entropy, close to the dark borders of the eventual energy-death of all Creation?

In his wildest dreams, Thane did not find the answer. Instead, he drifted off to sleep with Illara's haunting face hovering in his mind.

And the ship drove on toward its strange, unhallowed goal at the edge of time.

10 TO THE DARK WORLD

It was a strangely mismatched company who set forth on the Quest of the Time Treasure in Prince Chan's sleek yacht. Thane observed his companions with wry humor, oddly amused by the quirk of fate that had set such very different people together in this mad journey to the edge of infinite time . . .

There was Chan himself, the albino princeling from Shimar in the Dragon Stars, Chan with his cold, inscrutable eyes and bland face . . . Chan, whose heart was a black furnace wherein raged intolerable fires of greed, ambition and supernal pride.

And there was Shastar, rough bandit chieftain of the Red Moon of Phiolanthe, swaggering, blustering Shastar, burly as a bull, his hook-nosed face and blazing golden beard . . . bluff, rugged, bellowing Shastar who faced life with an oath on his lips, a swordblade in one mighty hand and a tankard of red wine in the other.

Thane's lips twitched, thinking of the strange fate that had bound two such different men together. For Chan was all ice and steel—Shastar all fire and flash. Chan's way was the dagger in the back, the sly whispered insinuation, the venom on the dart, the posion in the cup. But Shastar was a fighting man: set him face to face with a foe, sword in hand, and he was in his element. Confront him with a war fought with assassins and spies, with falsehoods and tricks, and he was obscurely uncomfortable.

Such was the situation on the moment. When Chan's ship dropped down through the red sky over the moon castle and took aboard the chieftain and a crew of his warriors, Thane noted how uncomfortable the yellow beard was in his presence. And Thane could tell that Shastar was his kind of man, bluff and hearty and straightforward. In fact, he guessed that Shastar hated and feared Chan, who was his ally, while feeling a grudging admiration for Thane, who was (or had been, until recently) his enemy—the honest friendship between warrior and warrior.

Thane noted this, and tucked it away for further thought. It was a chink in the armor of his enemies, through which he yet might find a way to strike.

And then there was Illara . . . what part had she to play in the last act of this drama? Thane did not know whether he hated her, or . . . felt another emotion for the girl who had lied to him and betrayed him into the hands of his enemies. He knew he had been close to loving her. He felt she had been nearly in love with him . . . and then he discovered the falsehood at the heart of their bond . . . now he was at a loss to name the strange ambivalent feeling he felt for the slim girl. Her beauty still had fire and wine in it, still could move him to passion, to fierce hungry wanting . . . but how can love be built on lies and deceptions?

She avoided him whenever she might, her eyes refused to meet his, and she shrunk back whenever he came near her. What was her relationship to Chan, her master? She was his slave, his tool . . . was he her lover? Did she serve the cold Prince through passion, or through fear? Somehow, Thane could not bring himself to think she felt ought but fear and loathing for the albino. And he felt certain Chan felt nothing for women—his secret reptilian heart could lust only for wealth, power and the mastery of others . . .

So these mismatched people, bound together by the bonds of their mutual quest, yet divided by fear, hatred and suspicion, drove on through the dark void to their far goal. Thane, bitter and betrayed, alone in the midst of foes, stayed to himself, kept his face closed and blank and his manner cool. It would yet be seen how the last act of this drama was to be played. He awaited it with curiosity and a sense of mockery . . .

Mnom lies far to the galactic north in the fringe of the Near Stars of central Carina-Cygnus, on the very edge of the Black Nebula. Its primary, Ghondaloom, is a dim Red Giant with a K5 spectrum similar to Aldebaran, and, like that star, some fifty times larger than Sol. Ghondaloom has only two planets, and its system is one of the oddest freaks in all of the Near Stars.

The first planet is Yinglara, the Planet of Light, whose orbit is close about the glaring red titan which burns against the spiderlike cloud of darkness that is the Black Nebula like a last, lone beacon fire against the ramparts of Eternal Night.

But Yinglara's companion world, dark Mnom circles

forever in a matched orbit. It floats through space perpetually in the shadow of the bright planet and never sees its parent star. Like some cosmic allegory of Good and Evil locked in unending combat and unending balance, the Planet of Light and the Dark World circle the glowing red eye of weird Ghondaloom there on the edge of the Black Nebula.

The Yacht floated through the dark void bearing its crew of men and women, with all their passions and thirsts, their hatred and suspicion and the tensions that these generated. They slept and ate, and slept again, and little converse passed between them on this lonely voyage to the edge of known space. Thane had little opportunity to speak to the girl even if he had wished to do so, for she kept herself apart from him and never looked at him except when she thought he was not noticing. But often he felt the urgency of her dim purple gaze upon him, questioningly; sadly haunted eyes filled with shadows of sorrow over something that might have been. But when he looked up, her eyes were turned away, and he would smile bitterly, mockingly, and call for wine.

And ever Chan was near, his cold ruby eyes observing with subtle humor and delicious malice the fruits of his little comedy of lies. He often smiled at Thane who pretended Illara meant nothing to him, and there was in his smile a knowing, poisonous mockery, a sense of things known but unspoken, of a heart cold as iron and forever locked against the warmer emotions, and hence a heart that rejoiced in the sour, sterile wine of its superiority. And Thane hungered to feel that white throat between his hands, and to see those cold red eyes goggling with terror and begging for life.

But he said nothing, he only grinned and drank wine, and vowed that his day would come. In the meantime, he kept silent, and watched, and waited . . .

Once when Shastar was at the control console alone, Thane wandered in and asked the burly bandit how soon they would arrive at the haunted planet of perpetual shadow. Shastar turned a flushed face and guilty eyes to meet his cool, questioning gaze.

"Soon enough. Days, now . . . two; three at the most. Ah, swordsman! I—" the bluff old pirate grimaced. "By Arnam's Beard and Thaxis' Spear, I've never asked a warrior's pardon ere now in all my days, but . . ."

Thane smiled slightly and clapped him on the shoulder.

"I think I know, chieftain—you need not say it. It was not the way you would have fought, was it?"

Shastar swore feelingly.

"Gods of Space, *no!* Put a sword in my hand and set me within arms' reach of a man, and my heart's easy, whether I win or lose the fight! But this, this tangle of lies and play-acting, *faugh*—it's the way women and eunuchs fight, not—*men.*"

Thane shrugged.

"I know. You and I are very much alike. Say no more . . ." But Shastar was not done. Flushing, he groped for words that were not in his rude vocabulary.

"And . . . and the wench, swordsman! Don't blame her for what happened. The lass was enmeshed in this foul tangle, the same as I . . ."

Thane lost his smile. His eyes went cold.

"Perhaps . . . perhaps not. But all I know was that she had a choice there on the stolen spaceboat. She did not *have* to draw that paralysis gun and beam me down . . . we were well on our way to escaping from both of you . . . we could have been free, but for her . . . *loyalty* . . . to her snake-hearted master."

"No! You're wrong there, too, swordsman! The girl had even less choice in the matter than did I," Shastar protested. Thane turned curious eyes on him.

"How so—*less* choice?"

Shastar growled, hunching burly shoulders beneath his cloak of fur.

"Some devil's trick . . . some black sorcery fetched by Druu from his Black Planet! That yellow dwarf brought Chan the secret of some dark art by which he could enchain her mind and very will! I know not how 'twas done . . . some mummery with staring into glittering crystals and murmured words . . . but, however, the albino laid the impress of his will upon her, stamped his commands deep in her unconscious mind."

Thane had never heard of hypnosis, but the notion of this uncanny art by which the unscrupulous could enslave the mind as well as the body stirred his nape hairs, sent a chill through his blood, and awoke superstitious dread within his barbaric heart.

"*What* . . . commands?" he asked.

"That when she was to hear Chan's voice repeat a certain phrase, she was to beam you down with the paralysis gun," Shastar rumbled earnestly, his fierce eyes searching Thane's face. "Believe me, lad, when she heard those key words, Chan's impressed will superceded her own wishes. The wench was naught but a mindless automaton when she pulled out that pistol and smote you with its ray! Blame *her* not, for it was Chan's will working through the lass that worked betrayal on you!"

Slowly, Thane asked: "How do *you* come to know of this?"

Shastar met his eyes honestly.

"I'm his partner. The albino snake hid nothing from me. I liked it not, knowing you loved the wench, but what could I say? I want the treasure trove as much as Chan wants it—and only you hold the key to it. It's not *my* way of fighting, the Gods know, but what can I say? We are all in Zargon's Balance, lad. Judge me as you will . . . but I wanted you to know the truth about the wench . . ."

He strode out of the control cabin, leaving Thane alone. Alone with his thoughts and his decisions, and with some new matter to chew over in his mind.

And ahead of them the red spark of Ghondaloom grew ever brighter and larger in the scopes, as the hurtling ship clove the dark void like a silver arrow. The Dark World hove ever closer . . . and the five within the vessel drew ever nearer to the final, eventual showdown that would come at the conclusion of their strange quest.

None of them could guess at the strange doom that each would find, there in the Tower at the Edge of Time . . .

11 PLANET OF ETERNAL NIGHT

AT LAST the black shield of Mnom swelled in their scopes until it blocked the sky before them. It was like some gigantic sphere of polished ebony, and sight strained hopelessly striving to penetrate its mysteries. Thane remembered his stay on Mnom as if it were but yesterday . . . the strange Temple City with its walls and bastions of black marble and dark streets wherethrough robed and hooded priests moved on cryptic errands . . . the gigantic idols of the Aealim looming up limb by limb into a dark sky devoid of stars or moons . . . the weird step pyramids of the Time Temple wherein silent men guarded forever the strange relics of a lost race that had come and dwelt and ruled and passed away long ages before human history was born . . .

Strange and alien was this Dark World of the Time Priests, and no fit world for men to dwell upon. Men need light and warmth, the rugged strength of green woods and rolling hills under a sky filled with the benison of golden light. Men need blue seas and white-capped waves whereon to quest in tall ships. Not for humankind are these black haunted hills and weird woods, and not for mortal flesh the strange black seas of lightless Mnom, floating through everlasting darkness . . .

They came down far to the north of the Temple City, drifting to planetfall on a cinder plain ringed in with black cliffs in a rough land of stone and sand. Somewhere in these hills was hidden that curious gate between the ages called the Web of the Aealim, and they had only Chan's vague directions to guide them in seeking it. So they started on their journey, with pack animals laden with supplies, and a rough map sketched years ago by a renegade Time Priest, for which Chan had paid in heavy gold.

Sand like black crystals crunched beneath their boots as they climbed the crumbling hills. Above them brooded the black sky and all about loomed cliffs and crags, ghostly shapes wrapped in dense shadows. As they climbed, they came to realize that Mnom has, after all, the gift of light. For a faint and ghostly illumination gradually sketched in the details of the grim landscape about them . . . slowly, as their eyes became accustomed to the darkness, they sensed a dim radiance from the sky, like the faintest shadows of distant light, vague and almost invisible.

It was uncanny, this ghost of radiance. Illara, bundled in a robe of furs against the chill thin air, shivered as she stared around at the bleak world.

"How can anyone live here in all this darkness?" she whispered faintly. Chan, a dimly white figure looming through the dark, laughed coldly.

"Men can live under the most grim conditions," he observed mockingly. "They never cease to hope for better times to come." His eyes, colorless as crystal in

the dimness, glanced at the silent Thane and then at
the shuddering girl. "Aye, hope lives on in the face of
all betrayal . . . in the stark jaws of iron Truth, men
still hope for joy and warmth and love," he smiled.

"He who does not hope," Thane said grimly, "is a
dead man."

Prince Chan's only reply was a mocking laugh.

They climbed on for hours until, weary with a bone
deep exhaustion, they gathered in the shelter of the
black cliffs and built a small fire and rested while
Shastar's men hastily threw together a rough meal.

They ate the rude fare in silence, together yet
apart, unspeaking as even the faint ghost of radiance
vanished and utter blackness closed in like a wall of
blindness. Then, leaving Shastar's lieutenant, Gorshang, to arrange a guard, they retired for the night.
Thermal tents of rubbery, heat-retaining substance
were erected in the shelter of the cliff wall, one tent
for each of them. Thane wrapped his great blue cloak
about him in the close warmth of the little tent, and
soon drifted into a dreamless but uneasy sleep. His
were the blunt nerves of a barbarian, accustomed to
hardship and deprivation and used to perils. The barbarian can be comfortable wherever he is; he never
worries for the dangers of the morrow; he can sleep
soundly on the very brink of Hell. Yet Thane's dreams
were disturbed by curious threads of thought that
wove through his sleeping brain like half-heard voices
whispering from the depths of time . . . he rolled and
tossed uneasily, his mind filled with disturbing pre-
monitions and half-sensed warnings . . . he slept ill,
and woke in a bad temper to find a black and sunless
'dawn.'

They pushed on into the mountains. The air became thin and cold as the blade of a fencing sword; it bit at their lungs and dried their lips and turned their warm breath into clouds of minute ice crystals. The strain of endless climbing wore down their strength in small subtle ways, frayed the edges of their temper, clawed at the precarious calm of their minds. They became touchy and quarrels exploded furiously into raging life at the slightest word or act. Shastar was forever striding among his men, thundering oaths and laying around him with a broadsword's flat blade, keeping the peace by heavy threats and a heavier hand.

Thane remained silent and aloof from the others. Chan tried to needle him into open rebellion, but the warrior ignored him, and at last the Prince was forced to turn to Druu for satisfaction of his small sadisms. He flayed the hunchbacked little sorceror endlessly, teasing him with clever words and jests. Thane watched, broodingly, and said nothing. As for the dwarf, he sought to keep his temper, but his slitted cold eyes snapped with frosty venom and his clawed hands strayed often to his dagger hilt. Thane thought it would take but little to goad the withered little enchanter into driving that crooked blade beween Chan's shoulders. Chan sensed this too, but was amused by the possibility of danger, and continued baiting the dwarf with honeyed, mocking, poisonous words. He was like a man who owned a dangerous pet, and loved to tease it to the very brink of striking at him.

Yet Druu never struck.

Perhaps he was biding his time, even as Thane was. Waiting for the perfect moment to strike and to rid himself once and for all of a master whose cruelty and arrogance he hated, and of whom he went ever in the cold grip of perpetual fear. It was a tense, explosive situation, and Thane enjoyed it. His own time had not yet come. He smiled in the half-darkness, wondering if the yellow dwarf from Yoth Zembis would someday explode, and perform Thane's vengeance for him.

Mnom was clad in eternal darkness, but life ever strives to combat the conditions under which it must exist. And even here in these barren rocks, amid these stark cliffs and black walls, life struggled for existence. Flying things went over their heads sometimes through dark skies; gaunt dragon hawks with croaking cries, their long snakelike bodies clad in glittering serpent scales, flying on flapping batlike wings. Occasionally a great lizard with moony eyes like luminous opals and flickering tongue that tasted their scent on the chill air, watched them pass below from high nests amidst the crags.

And there were even plants amid this barren desert of black marble cliffs and crystal sands . . . the strange fire-flowers of Mnom that glowed phosphorescently against the night in eternal protest against darkness. Weird they were, these ghost flowers that bloomed amid dead stones . . . phosphor roses burned green and gold, and there were fire lilies of pallid cream and milky blue flame . . . weird and terrible, yet with a haunting beauty to them that made even their glowing presence welcome to eyes that hungered for light. Shastar, clumsy in his chivalry, plucked a sheaf of fire flowers and handed them silently to Illara. She held them against her breast and

Thane could see how their strange luminance lit her face with witch fires of ghostly green, glowing in the depths of her eyes. Silently, her haunted face stared at him through the murk, painted against the black canvas of eternal night with magic pigments of liquid flame.

Still he did not speak to her, nor did she speak to him. They had built a wall of silence between them, raising it brick by brick, and neither would be the first to breach it, although, perhaps, both of them wished that it were not there.

She went on without speaking, but she kept the glowing flowers for hours, until at last their witch fires faded and died and her face was a mask of shadows again.

At last, on the third day of their trek, they reached the top of a great plateau that lay all bare black stone, clean and sterile under the cold gusts of wind that swept it. No ship could land here, for the plateau was thronged with needle spires of black rock that thrust up at the grim sky like the bared fangs of some tremendous dragon. The wind sang through the forest of stone spires with an eerie and never-ending song that tore at the nerves and plucked with fingers of dim madness at the threshold of the mind. It was like the shadowy cry and sobbing song of ghosts tormented endlessly in some black and icy hell of frozen stone.

And there before them lay the Temple of the Time Web.

It was builded of rough slabs of black stone, crudely hewn from the cliffs about and welded together by some unguessable magic fire. Grim and stark it loomed amidst the petrified needles, a square cube of darkness, devoid of ornament or carving. Nothing broke the rudely hacked planes of its black stone walls but a single door which stood open and yawned like the eyehole of a skull.

Shastar's warriors huddled against the spires and eyed the crypt dubiously, whispering among themselves, their eyes glinting fearfully in the light of Chan's torch. They were reluctant to advance any closer to the grim structure, but Chan toyed with the jeweled hilt of his electric whip and Shastar's bellowing voice drove them on.

As they approached the temple, the crying voices in the wind sang louder and nearer . . . as if trying to warn them of danger. Like ghosts sobbing from the borders of another world, whispering across the vastness of that unguessable abyss which yawns between the world of Life and the black world of Death. Shastar grumbled a curse, and superstitiously fingered an amulet of blue paste devised in the benign likeness of Maryash the Protector, which dangled about his bull-like throat beneath his heavy furs.

As for the reptilian zimdars that carried the packs, the beasts refused to advance another step toward the grim crypt with its shadowy, yawning door. They hissed and struck, long snaky necks flashing. There was nothing to do but tether the beasts here while the humans went on ahead.

Chan was the first to reach the door of the shrine. He flashed his light within, then turned and gestured the others in. Crossing the high stoop, Illara stumbled and Thane, who was directly behind her, caught her arm and steadied her.

"Thank you . . ." she murmured, turning. Her

voice stuck and she was silent when she saw whose hand had helped her over the step.

"That's all right," he said quietly. For a moment he held her gaze, wishing he could think of something to say, but although words trembled on the threshold of speech, he was silent. Her eyes were enormous wells of purple shadow, haunted with unspoken sadness; they looked at him for a moment, while her soft lips parted breathlessly, then her gaze wavered and fell, and she stepped away from him, entering into the dense gloom of the building.

Cursing himself for a tongue-tied idiot, he stumbled after her. Behind him came Shastar and the little dwarf, still lugging the device that dampened Thane's mind powers.

Once within, the five halted and looked around while Chan's beam quested the dense shadows.

The room was like a great cube hollowed out of solid stone. Its interior was as barren of ornament or carvings as had been the outside walls. Their footsteps rang and echoed in the musty cold air.

"There!" Chan said suddenly.

Thane looked—and caught his breath in wonder.

In the very center of the chamber of black stone a vast frame of brass hung suspended from the roof, hidden above in century-thick shadows. The brass sparkled redly in the electric ray. And within the frame . . . filling it from side to side, from top to bottom, was . . . the Web.

Thane felt his flesh crawl as he stared at it.

Imagine a ghostly film of darkness that moved with hidden writhings . . . a web spun of shadow substance, like a veil of dark mist . . . whorls and spirals of darkness that coiled and writhed with a serpentine motion, restless as tendrils of shadowy smoke. It chilled the blood with its suggestion of something that *lived*, yet slept . . . a tangle of vaporous serpents, sluggishly twining . . . a screen of coiling smoke, endlessly in motion, half alive . . . and the knowledge that this frame of brass had been set here by inhuman, alien hands a thousand million years ago and more . . . that alien hands had woven this dark web of time stuff before man first rose from his haunches in some dark primeval jungle and stood erect and gazed up wonderingly at the stars . . .

"Let us begin."

Chan's cold phrase cut through the tangle of Thane's unspoken thoughts. He felt the others turn and gaze at him, and knew that they had at last come to the moment when his unknown powers must be proved. Now he must pit his brain against the Time Wizards of the Fire Mist. Now he must either do . . . or fail.

The waiting was over; the time to act had come.

But *could* a mere human mind arouse this web of dark forces that had slept here for a billion years or more? Could he trigger the sleeping powers of this gate of strange magic that linked the Future with the Past?

Could he or any man employ the instruments of an alien and age old science?

He knew with stark certainty that if he tried and could not, then he was a dead man. For Chan's fingers toyed lovingly with the hilt of his coagulator, and Thane stood only seconds from the finality of death.

Behind him somewhere, he heard Illara sharply draw in her breath. And Shastar muttered something under his breath—a curse?—a prayer?—perhaps both in one.

"I said, let us begin. Druu, shut off that thing and give this man back his mind," Chan said coldly.

Standing there alone he heard the yellow dwarf tinkering with the electronic dampener. He heard its omnipresent drone die. He heard silence, heavy as a leaden weight.

And his mind came alive again!

Thrilling beyond all words, that surge of inner power! Sudden clarity of vision drove away the mists that had enshrouded his brain for so long that he had gotten used to being only half-alive, mentally. Now his keen mind probed out with strange senses, tasting the air, feeling the cold rough stone, smelling the dust of centuries in this shadow-fraught tomb.

He drew in his breath, drunk with the exhilaration of power—power that he alone possessed, of all men alive in this hour! Power such as no being had exerted for all the long history of Man! *Power that was his alone—power that he shared only with a lost race of forgotten gods!*

And he stepped forward to the very threshold of the Web . . . and he raised his arms . . .

12 THE WEB OF THE AGES

HE STOOD, a bronzed, heroic figure with legs wide-spread and bare, muscular arms raised before the Web, and his mind quested within its shadowy depths. His head was flung back, the long fiery mane pouring over his vast blue cloak like a torrent of blood, and his mind reached out, groping within the swirling mists . . . sensors probed . . . impinged on something almost, but not quite, tangible, a shape of force that yielded to his mind tendril. He probed at its pseudosurface, entered it like a key going into a lock . . . *and the Web opened before them!*

The shadowy film of crawling darkness that was woven between the four angles of the brass frame pulsed now with swifter life! The vaporous coils of impalpable time stuff swirled about—sank inward—and they fell into and down a whirling vortex of darkness that roared in their ears!

Chan cried out a wordless paean of triumph—Illara shrieked—Shastar boomed out a defiant war cry—Druu gibbered with terror—of the five, only Thane did not give voice to his emotions: his mind was drenched with sheer awe at the stupendous vista of

receding ages that opened out before them as they
passed into the Web . . .

Within a second the five figures vanished and the
film of shadows slowed . . . and slept again, for all
the world as if its aeon-deep slumber had never been
broken. There were left behind only Gorshang and
the other warriors, gaping with astonishment, grasp-
ing amulets, kneeling on the dusty pave in primal terror. They were left behind, with the darkness and the
crying wind, alone.

With some sight beyond sight, in some manner that
transcended the physical limitations of fleshly sense,
they saw the future unfold before them in all its
countless billion convolutions. Their bodies seemed
consumed, destroyed, broken down to subatomic particles and dispersed as they were wafted forward on
the time winds that blew between the ages. They
could peer into the minds and hearts of a thousand
men in a single flashing instant—gaze at scenes tran-
spiring simultaneously on a hundred planets—read
meaning into the very texture of thought. It was fantastic, inhuman, godlike—exhilarating in the madness
and intoxication of the Power that was theirs alone to
glory in. Like gods, they bestrode the narrow centuries, sweeping on from world to world, from age to
age, in the aura of irresistible mastery and splendor
that glowed about them like living light.

The experience was to be forever stamped deep
within them, impressed in blood and brain and bone.
Never were they to forget this timeless moment beyond time when the radiance and power of the gods
were theirs.

First, they saw the near future . . .

They watched as the White Wizards of Parlion clashed in magic wars against the evil sorcerors of Yoth Zembis the Black Planet . . . they saw the Red Witch of Altair cast out her webs of wizardry and enslave minds and worlds to her dark empery.

They watched as the New Empire arose from Valdamar to replace the Old Empire that had broken and collapsed a thousand years in the past . . . they saw the proud Sons of Calastor lead the bright, steel-clad legions from the Nucleus World of the New Empire in wars of conquest that spread from star to star like a sheet of flame.

Before their dazed and astonished eyes, Torje and the Star Crusaders carried forward the starburst banners of Valdamar in savage struggles against the Machine Kings of Atrogon the Robot Planet . . . and the Sky Lords of Bartosca, who enslaved the Tigermen with their will-destroying death drug . . . watched as they battled the dread science of the Sun-Stealers of Arlomma the Ice Planet, and fought against the Mind Masters of Pelizon.

As they gazed, an incredible panorama of interstellar battles unfolded before them. They saw fleets of heroes, armed and armored with the weird science of the future, locked in combat with strange enemies on a hundred worlds—the Space Hag, with her terrible armies of the living dead, and the Red Slavers of the Demon Stars who spread out their light-league-wide gravity nets to ensnare the bright fleets, and the Black Dragons of Nephog Quun with their uncanny power to control the future.

They saw the bold Warrior Emperors sally forth with their glittering armadas, the heroic Phascalon of the Legions, and young Hajandir, Zarlon of the Star

Sword and Androthar . . . they watched the New Empire grow, and spread, and . . . change.

While they observed the unfolding ages, the long lost science of the Old Empire was reborn. Ships sped between the stars like flashing steel needles, weaving together the scattered planet kingdoms of the galaxy into a mighty Imperial tapestry. They saw men probe into the mystery of matter, peering deep into the complex hearts of spinning atoms, and one by one puzzle out and define the secrets of gravity, and space, and thought, and time itself. With stupendous lenses built of impalpable magnetic force fields, men magnified their vision and peered to the very limits of the expanding universe. And, over ages, arm after arm of the great galaxy was explored and mapped and settled and made part of the Empire, and man began to remake the Universe to his suiting. Artificial planets were steered into orbits about suns, drawing in by billion-erg gulps the measureless energy of heat . . . transmuting this power by continent-sized cell banks of dielectric accumulators, and spearing the sunpower forth in mighty beams of incredible force that tore planets into fragments, demolished unwanted moons, swept space clear of meteor swarms and asteroid belts. They saw the dome cities rise on airless worlds, bubbles of armor glass that sparkled amid the long ink-black shadows traced on the ash-white moonscapes along their daylight terminators. They saw the Empire change into new forms . . . the League of Thirty Suns . . . the Autarchate of the Orion Worlds . . . the galaxy swarmed with new races and nations; new religions and philosophies arose . . . and they stared without comprehension at the eras of the Ethical Triumvirs and the Triadic

Centralists, and the Twelve Hegemons of Aryx . . . they traced the rise of the High Dynasts of Trix, and the Nnermite Dissenters, and other forces and movements beyond naming rose and fell in the endless tides of centuries that sped past their superphysical vision.

Great fleets of nomad planets steered on magnetic flux, venturing beyond the great Home Galaxy of man to the neighboring island galaxies of Sculptor and Fornax, the three Leonid galaxies, the Greater and Lesser Magellanic Clouds, and even to far Andromeda, that mighty whirlpool of suns that lies a million and a half light-years from the Home Galaxy. These planetary armadas voyaged into the dark abyss of intergalactic space complete with suns to warm them; they would not reach their unthinkably distant goals for scores of centuries to come . . .

The Serrelian Enigma was created, and the five time travelers observed the Enigmatists and their long struggle against the dominance of the Starmasters of Anthlamar . . . then came the terrible age of invasion from the Andromeda Galaxy, and in all its endless horror, they watched The Fifty-Two Thousand Year War drain the strength and science from an exhausted galaxy until at last the Mind Bomb sterilized the enemy galaxy of its insectoid Ssu Entity and peace came down over a ruined, exhausted civilization, and technology ebbed and was forgotten as Mankind passed into the Pastoral Age that lasted half a million years.

The proud Era of the Kaspenfells passed by, and the epoch of the Astromancers. They watched the bitter wars of the Dional Moralists against the tyrannical megacities of The Hierarchate. The Aeon of the Gray

Magicians crept slowly by their enthralled vision, and they saw the reign of the Robot Philosophers of Niomakh, and the fall of the Nine Hegemons of Dex before the coming of Zor of the Seven Thousand Years . . . ages beyond thought, empires beyond name or number, swept past their dazed vision in a stupendous panorama of unending time . . .

Man evolved into higher, different forms, such as the Brainmen of Valthoth, and the Aathoklaa, and The Men Who Do Not Speak, and the Double-Men of Niovoth . . . then down on the evolved supermen of the very distant future came Azlak the Scarlet One, and the darkness of the long Barbarian Centuries obscured the passage of time . . . and they watched as the long-prophesied coming of Iom the Liberator brought light out of the darkness, and the long golden ages of Mankind's serene old age swept grandly past with its garden worlds and white marble cities . . . and the Universe was ruled wisely and well by the supernal minds of the Tensors of Pluron who had guided Mankind secretly for so many ages . . . and they watched the Golden Age of Kargon, and the epoch of the Mind Magicians, and the Aeon of the Eternal Men came . . . and passed . . . and then the Last Days were come down upon the star worlds.

They watched a Universe die . . .

For the stars that composed the Seventeen Galaxies dominated by the Congress of Human Civilizations were . . . old . . . *old* . . . ten billion years had passed as this cycle of the Plenum slid past. Even the ageless stars are not eternal, as the great scientists of this far distant age knew well. And those whose duty it was to Guard the Stars noted the first signs of senescence in the flickering, reddening radiation from suns once young and bright with strength and vigor.

Strange it was, to think that magnificent stars whose flashing rays outlast whole geological epochs of planetary life, are themselves prey to old age and death! Strange, to think of mighty suns falling into hoary desuetude, but it was so. While solemn mages, inhumanly evolved into new forms of eternal pseudo-flesh, pondered and wrought weird new philosophies beyond their primitive comprehension, or composed telepathic symphonies, or sculpted with planes of force entire planets into Sculptospheres of alien artistry . . . the suns were dying, one by one. Stars that had been white and fiercely burning and young when this strange odyssey into the farthest depths of time began, burned through warm yellow and rich gold, into deep, cooling crimson . . . black sunspots, like unthinkably stupendous scabs, obscured the surface of their ebbing fires . . . and sun after sun blackened and died.

In desperate attempts to rekindle the dying star fires, entire planets were manipulated in grapnels of impalpable force, and flung into the cooling embers of the stars. For a time, the old stars burned fresh and fierce anew, but at length even these methods failed, and the multishaped alien men of that far age despaired and died, or fled afar to younger galaxies.

One by one, the stars went out and the mighty galaxy darkened. World after world was deserted by its people, as, wrapped in envelopes of force, they flew by thought power to far off havens. World after world was caught in the grip of the ice demons of the interstellar cold . . . their atmospheres crystallized in decade-long snows of frozen oxygen . . . world after world that had once been young and gay and filled with life and purpose, slept out Eternity locked under miles of frigid ice.

And Man . . . passed.

Untenanted, empty of life, the dead galaxy revolved in its slow cycle, turning over in black space like an inconceivable pinwheel revolving, and each vast revolution consumed one hundred million years of time. Its last fires dying, the stupendous vortex of darkening suns revolved on . . . ever and ever slower now . . . slower . . .

And *stopped*.

The dead galaxy broke apart in the grip of tidal forces of unthinkable immensity. No longer did the vast centrifugal force of the revolving star wheel hold the galactic star drifts in shape—they were flung widely apart. Frozen worlds were dislodged from their orbits with gigantic force. The burned out cinders of dead stars fell from their stations—cracked apart—shattered into fragments—or thundered together in frightful cosmic collisions that awoke within the still warm cores of many one last phoenix flame of thermonuclear fury.

It was a spectacle such as the mind of man has rarely depicted or imagined: whole star clusters were ripped out of place amid the galactic arms, as those arms themselves disintegrated under titanic tidal drag —tens of thousands of planets and stars came together in supernova collisions whose unimaginable impact ripped and tore at the very fabric of space time itself.

Then . . . at last, all was still, the last fires dying. The dead ruins of a broken galaxy floated in the utter darkness of cosmic space as the predestined energy death of the Universe . . . the final limbo of balanced entropy . . . approached on slow and silent wings.

Viewing the end of the glorious and yet tragic pageant of Mankind's mighty epic, Thane felt exaltation fill him. It roared with godlike intoxication through his veins like heady wine—

"Hai—Gods of Time! Aye, but it was worth the toil of living to see what we have seen—to have traversed the gulf of unthinkable billions of years that no mortals save we few have ever spanned—and to come to the last dim edge of Eternity—the last human beings alive in all the Universe! Gods! If I die now, let it be said by warriors and sung by the bards of my home world that I, Thane of Zha, have—lived!"

13 THE SCARLET TOWER

THE FIVE time travelers had all but lost their senses of individual consciousness during the timeless interval while they sped on wings of thought through the unfolding ages of the far future and viewed the stupendous panorama of billions on billions of years of time. Lost in the spectacle, they had forgotten *themselves!*

But now the numbing pageant was over—now the age long saga of Mankind's incredible destiny was ended, with all its complexity of empires and epochs, worlds and ages. Like enthralled spectators caught up and held helpless in the grip of some supernal drama written by a Master Demiurge, who slowly and painfully awaken into their private worlds again once the last act is played, the curtain falls and the houselights burn brightly again, the time travelers came to themselves slowly, one by one.

And became aware that their incredible quest through a million ages was very nearly at its end.

Their forward flight through time had ended; no more they sensed that vertiginous rush through the centuries, borne on unseen wings of time.

Now they seemed to hover—to float in lightless space at the very brink of Eternal Nothingness.

Their physical bodies were still dispersed clouds of force, but they found they could in some unknown manner between the known senses communicate one with the other.

Thane pointed mentally.

"Look!"

Their sense of perception followed the direction of his unseen guidance, and they saw their goal approaching.

Up out of the abyss of frozen darkness there slowly swam toward them where they hovered aloft—one lone and last still-burning star!

Like a drifting spark of light drowned and lost amidst an inconceivable abyss of darkness, its minute and lonely point of radiance seemed ineffably sad, unbearably pitiful. From all the glittering, sun-thronged hosts of a million galaxies of dazzling stars . . . one last fugitive spark of vanished splendor persisted on the black brink of the cosmos. Perhaps the fury of that cosmic collision of crashing suns, when the dying galaxy slowed and disintegrated, had triggered within its core one last surge of thermonuclear fires. Or perhaps it was merely the last born of the stars, and the last to die . . . but there, alone against the illimitable dark, one faint red spark yet flickered . . . flickered near to its own extinction, yet still, for a time, it lived.

The timeless rush of their flight slowed as this last star swam up toward them. They saw circling in lonely orbit about the red star, the Last Planet.

And they knew that it was here the ancient Aealim had raised the Tower Beyond Time.

They fell toward the Last Planet, watching it grow

and grow beneath them until it filled half the dark sky. It has been, perhaps, a dead world, frozen deep beneath its blankets of frozen oxygen, before the sun torch had been rekindled. For it was barren and sere, a featureless desert of ash grey sand, through which pierced here and there the worn down stumps of ancient mountains whose sharp peaks had been abraded away by remorseless centuries of wind and rain, sun and snow.

Dead sea bottoms stretched from lifeless pole to lifeless pole, and a thin cold wind whispered across the sunken plains where once, a billion years before, fierce winds had driven mighty waves of green water. Now there was only a faint whispering sigh of wind sounding here, as like some mocking echo of vanished seas. . . .

Like bodiless ghosts nearing some planet of the dead, the five travelers drifted over the ashen landscape that was but dimly lit by the cooling rays of a dull red sun.

They floated over the ruined shell of a city whose builders had died or passed on to newer, other worlds geological epochs ago. A strange, nameless city of the farthest future it was, constructed of some time-resisting stuff that was neither ceramic nor plastic, but lustrous and pale, like ancient ivory or old worn porcelain.

Earthquakes had toppled the tall towers and broken down the walls and crushed the swelling domes flat. The streets were empty of everything but sighing wind and blown dust and silent shadows. Once, these broad avenues had teemed with life and motion, with fast glittering vehicles riding on magnetic currents, with strange future folk in bright garments of newly invented colors. No more. . . .

The Last City drifted away under them and was gone across the turning curve of the dead world.

And then far ahead of them on a spur of the worn old mountains they glimpsed a flash of intense color, so strange and unexpected in all this world of grey that it hurt the senses to look upon it.

Scarlet it was, as fresh blood, and fashioned of some strange glassy substance that knew neither crack nor joinure. A weirdly shapen pinnacle atop the mountain crest, soaring against the dead black sky wherein the Last Sun still burned fitfully, feebly, soon to die.

Like the castle of some mad Enchanter, the minaret lifted its spires against the dark, crenelated and cloven after the fashion of some peculiar architecture unknown to men of their own far distant age. The last dim dying rays of the ancient sun drew lines of glittering red fire down the smooth glistening flanks of its seamless height.

They came down to a flat space that stretched before the Tower, and their bodies reassembled in some unknown fashion. No more time-wandering phantom clouds of disembodied thought, they stood before the Tower as flesh and blood again.

An icy wind plucked at the folds of Thane's great blue cloak and spread it like immense wings until he gathered it in about him against the knifelike chill. The blue fabric now glowed brownish purple in the weird crimson light of the half dead star. His fiery mane of hair glistened death black, and his bronzen gold hide was tinted a ghastly greenish copper.

Numbed by the strangeness of their mighty odyssey

through the abyss of unguessed and unnumbered aeons, the time travelers stared at each other for a moment in silence, white-faced, brooding over the gigantic saga whose ringing immortal cantos they had seen written on the scroll of time . . .

Illara shrank within her heavy furs, and the cold wind burned like fire on her white cheeks, where tear tracks glistened wetly. Shastar's flame-bearded head was bowed on his broad chest and his fierce hawk eyes were hooded, clouded with thought.

In Chan's deathly pale face, however, the same arrogance and lust for gold blazed with unquenched flame. Even the sight of that vast epic which stood as a stupendous metaphor for the utter futility of any attempt to build up and preserve anything against the remorseless erosion and final collapse of all striving—even the whole giant parable of man's mutability, failed to blunt the icy edge of his driving purpose.

He caught Thane's eye and gestured grimly to the scarlet shaft before them.

Thane grinned in mockery. *What use to covet loot, when even stars must die?*

The swordsman shook himself a little, hunching his shoulders against the keen chill in the thin air. He shrugged off the strange mood of exaltation that had seized him as he watched the Tale of Man unfold in all its grandeur and glory . . . and end in futility. Grimly, he set his jaw and lifted against the cold and threatening darkness of the sky above a great clenched fist, and shook it defiantly.

Unspoken thoughts welled within him. Against all the futility and tragic destiny of life, which is born but to decay and die, one purpose still leaped high within his unconquerable heart. If all were futile, if the end of all striving comes to naught—*at least we have the glory of having lived, and fought!*

"Be the end what it may—the rest of the tale is ours to glory in!" he thundered to the deaf, dead stars.

Chan stared at him wonderingly through the drifting cold. His ruby eyes were weeping, but only from the keen-edged wind. Chan's heart knew only greed, but there was within him enough intelligence to wonder before a man who could see all the uselessness of life, and still exult in the possessing of it.

They all stared at him through the icy wind, shuddering as it bit like sword edges of steel against bare arms and legs. Thane voiced a bitter laugh of self-mockery: he felt the intoxication ebb within him, the pride drained from his heart and mind, leaving his thoughts clear and cold. He smiled at Prince Chan.

Then he turned to the Tower that soared before them, standing like a bloodied sword buried hilt-dead in dead grey ash.

It was time for the last scene of their little drama . . .

Illara felt something catch at her heart. A cry of pleading rose to her lips, but was muted there. With half-parted lips, she turned as if to beg Thane to stop . . . one slim hand went out to him, but fell back before the futile gesture was completed. There was no use in it. No use in anything. . . .

Chan's cold, weeping eyes were fixed on Thane's broad back. One strong white hand clung like a dead thing emptied of blood to the handle of his laser gun. The remorseless urging of his driving lust still thrust him on.

Shastar viewed the Prince sourly. *His* thirst for gold had died within him, there in the infinite reaches of eternal time. He craved no treasure now, but the warmth and fullness of a contented life.

For him, at least, the quest was ended.

For Thane, too, the quest had ended. But, as yet, he did not realize it.

Chan stood behind him, the laser pistol clenched in his hand, eyes watering at the unbearable chill that bit clear to the bone, face tightly closed, eyes watchful . . .

Thane's mind probed out and pried into the nameless substance whereof the Aealim had builded their fortress against the ages. Probed and pried . . . sank into the seamless red material that was unlike anything man's hand had ever fashioned.

And suddenly a door opened before them in the unbroken wall of scarlet!

Solid substance melted into vapor and vanished into emptiness as Thane's mind caught the lock and opened it. Weird, weird it was, to watch the sheer magical swiftness with which the red stuff—be it plastic, or ceramic, or some unknown combination of the two—distingegrated into thin mist.

They stared into the open door, gazing into the yawning blackness of the portal.

With bitter mockery, Thane turned to the Prince who stood behind him.

"Now, my lord Prince, shall we go forward and look upon this treasure so rich and rare that we have dared the gulf of ages to find it?"

14 THE TIME TREASURE

CHAN was the first one through the door. Druu, the dwarfed enchanter from Yoth Zembis, was close on his heels, eyes glittering with excitement, and even Shastar followed. Illara exchanged a long look with Thane, and then they, too, went through the portal to stand within the Tower.

At first there was only a sensation of immensity: the crimson walls of the Time Tower soared straight up into remoteness and were lost overhead in clinging, age thick shadows. There were no rooms or chambers . . . just one vaulted, ceilingless hall. The immensity of the Tower could not be perceived from outside; within, it seemed far huger, like the magic castle of some Enchanter.

On top of the sensation of soaring immensity, you perceived shadowy dimness. The walls seemed oddly translucent, permitting light to pass through from beyond the Tower, but it was a dim red gloom, drowned with purple shadows like some dense fog.

Light grew stronger, clearer.

It was as if the walls were self-luminous. Or as if you stood within some giant's lamp made of that scar-

let alabaster the Tigermen hew from deep quarries on
far Bartosca, under the whips of the winged Sky
Lords who rule the Land of Fire. You stood amid a
strengthening, ever-brightening blaze of deep scarlet
illumination.

And then you saw the treasure . . .

The entire shaft of the giant structure was choked
with a flood of burning gold.

The precious metal glowed with ruby radiance in
all the crimson light. Gold . . . gold . . . everywhere
you turned, your eyes were filled with the glorious
luster of the rare metal. It was fashioned into crowns
and coronets, diadems and tiaras, helms and shields,
rings, armlets, brooches, batons, flagstaffs, thrones,
breastplates, idols, images, statues, busts, artworks.

Coins. Coins of a thousand ancient realms on a
hundred million worlds. Coins of gold, silver, plati-
num, bronze, nickel, *chaya*, iridium, and the precious
metals of many planets. Coins of bronze and silver
from luxurious Sybaris and Iberia, and glittering Syr-
acuse where wise Archimedes measured the earth;
gold staters incised with the profiles of Seleucid and
Antiochan monarchs with ivy-wreathed brows; silver
tetradrachms from Babylon, whereon the mighty Alexander had stamped his likeness with the accoutre-
ments of his ancestor, the god Hercules; coins from
antique Carthage minted in Iberian silver and
stamped with the pyramid and crescent of the goddess Tanit; Persian gold drachmai and Punic *Zeraa* of
red copper; silver wedges from the Etruscans and
bars of Numidian iron; gold denarii with the proud,
hook-nosed profiles of Roman Caesars; coins like but-
tons from Aegina, and coins like bars from Lacedae-
mon, and coins from Bactria shaped like tablets; elec-

trum coins from Tunis, and others from Aradus bearing the galley and hippocamp emblem; Persian darics
and sigloi; Greek talents and Moslem dinars; coins
oval or triangular, discoid or square, rectangular or
ring-shaped. A thousand thousand treasuries had been
emptied into this mighty vault!

And jewels. Indian diamonds, smoky as clouded
quartz. Black diamonds from Africa, dark as obsidian.
Opals, zircons, beryls, turquoises, sandastras, and
pearls like so many miniature moons. Necklaces of jet
and amber and porphyry. The three kinds of ruby,
and the four kinds of sapphire, and the twelve kinds
of emerald. Chalcedonies which guard against poison,
and amethysts which guard against drunkenness. Red
carbuncles, condensed from the urine of lynxes. To-
pazes, like lion's eyes. The gems blazed like pools of
liquid light, sparkling and glittering and sending out
their prisoned radiance in sheets and rays and sparks
and starry clusters.

The loot of Empires was here: the sack of Perse-
polis and golden Susa and Baghdad of the Caliphs;
the ransom of Montezuma and the treasure of Alexander and the wealth of Croesus! Here were elephant
tusks as long as a man is high, heaped upon lion-skins
from Mount Atlas, and silver urns filled with pow-
dered coral, and blocks of purest amber from the land
of the Hyperboreans. And here were barbaric plumes
of fantastic birds from Ethiopia bound with threads
of scarlet silk, and myrrh from Arabia Felix and fran-
kincense and balm, and odorous nard, saffron and
rare spices from Ceylon and the Isles of China, and
great bars of glowing orichalcum from fabled and
still-unfound Atlantis.

Bronze plates and sheets of thin gold, silver ingots

and cubes of jade; gold-dust in bottles of hippo hide
and peacock feathers from the Rajahs of India. Here
were amulets of paste and talismans of virgin copper,
scarabs of haematite and periapts of green jasper, all
in a litter of ivory spoons and spatulas of gold. Here
were the Hejet and the Deshen, the red and the white
Crowns of Upper and Lower Egypt—and the great
Pshent, the Double Crown. A priceless seed from
Zaqqum the Tree of Hell was here, set in a plaque of
pure silver; and a drop of water from the sacred
Zem-Zem, the Well of Life, in holy Mecca, set in the
hollow center of a yellow diamond.

It was the loot of many worlds, the treasures of the
Czars and the Ptolemies, the riches of imperial Babylon and Byzantium and the Golden Chersonese . . .
worked gold from Sardis and ebony from Egyptian
Thebes; the signet ring of Xerxes and the gold scarab
of Cleopatra; carnelian from Sogdiana and lapis la-
zuli from Chorasmia . . . inscribed tablets of red gold
from Chaldea and Sumer, Akkad and the realm of the
Hittites and the empire of the Assyrians.

The eye skimmed over it, drinking in the shaking
aura of golden radiance that played about it, and the
mind shrank back from attempting to measure it. For
the loot of many planets was here, and of all ages,
strange Martian statues of radioactive crystal and fantastic sphinx-headed idols from far stars, hewn from
gigantic jewels, and a million metals and gems and
rarities to which the five could give no name.

Truly, all the treasure of a Universe was heaped
and mounded in this vast room.

Chan was transfigured. Naked greed flamed in his
eyes and his mouth hung slack and open, working

wetly. He babbled and dropped to his knees, scrabbling about in the lakes of jewels and hills of coinage,
his gun forgotten.

Thane looked down at him cynically. And it was at
that very moment that doom came to Prince Chan
of Shimar, at the very height and pinnacle of his
triumph—

Perhaps the dwarf Druu had waited for this moment with patience and cunning, knowing how much
more dreadful to Chan would be that death which
struck him when he stood at last within arm's reach
of the thing he most wanted. Or it may be that the
lust of gold—the temptation of all this incredible
wealth spread out before him in its dazzling splendor
—tipped him over the edge. But however it came
about, this was the moment in which Druu struck
back at the cruel master who had taunted and tormented him for so many years—

Belching out some gobbling cry, whose words they
could not make out, the dwarfed enchanter struck at
Chan's bent back with a wicked hooked dagger. The
smacking sound the blade made when it went in was
clearly audible. It was like the slapping sound a
cleaver makes against cold meat.

Chan froze. His eyes glazed with shock, with the
sheer incredulity of the blow. His body straightened
slowly, jerkily, until he stood on his two feet. As he
turned around to see whose hand had struck him,
Thane, Shastar and Illara could see the hilt of the
dagger where it protruded from between his shoulders. Red blood dribbled down his back, staining the
white silk of his garments and glistening wetly in the
light of the Tower's alabastrine walls. All was silence.

He stared at Druu with mad eyes, eyes wherein the

cold ruby fires had at last been touched to heat. The dwarf was kneeling, cackling with hideous mocking laughter.

Chan's pallid mouth worked, but no words came out.

His two fists, clenched and white-knuckled, were crammed full with gems. Now his tendons slackened and the jewels clattered over the gold-strewn floor. With infinite slow care, one hand went to his hip and took the laser pistol from its jewel-set holster.

Druu groveled, shaking with demoniac mirth, laughing up into his master's face which glistened now with sweat. He spewed up laughter like phlegmy filth. He paid no attention to the gun that the Prince was lifting; his life had already accomplished its purpose, unlike Chan's; he had fully known and savored his moment of supreme, crowning triumph—

The searing needle of superheat cut him down. His face disappeared in the droning blast of the laser, and smoke bubbled up from the black pit that had been his face. He slid down the pile of gold, kicked once or twice with bowed legs, and was still. The echoes of his laughter still echoed around the red walls and gobbled in the dimness above, fading into silence.

Chan slowly turned a wet white face to stare at Thane and Illara. Muscles stood out like knotted cords at his temples. Great blobs of icy water studded his forehead and dribbled down his cheeks.

Then his shoulders sagged, as if the slight weight of the dagger were some heavy burden they could no longer bear up. His knees buckled, and he went down, sprawling amid the gold and the spilt gems that glittered like fresh clots of blood. His eyes glazed, still staring up but now blank and opaque, like rough marbles set in the wet white marble mask of his taut face.

And it was at that moment that madness struck them all.

For the heaped mounds of treasure, for which they had come so far . . . vanished!

15 THE CHILDREN OF THE FIRE MIST

THE GOLD MOUNTAINS evaporated into thin air. The jeweled crowns and mitres, idols, thrones and swords wavered on the air—became transparent—and were gone.

It was over in a single instant. They barely had time to notice it before it was accomplished.

Numbly, without comprehension, Shastar stared about him. Not so much as a single gem or a grain of dust remained. The floor was a single slab of red alabastrine substance, stretching from wall to wall without a speck of the treasure that had, moments before, almost completely hidden it from their sight.

The room was entirely empty, save for a rough hewn hexagonal block of smoky crystal against the far wall. This object they had not seen before; the treasure heaped about had hidden it from view. Now, simply because it was the only thing that remained beside themselves in the empty treasure vault, they stared at it.

And from it, came a whispering voice.

It seemed to speak to them across the span of immeasurable ages, faint yet clear, like a shadow of sound. Wise it was, and old, with a wisdom beyond that to which mortal flesh could ever aspire . . . and with an age so incredible that adamantine mountains could not sustain the piled centuries that the Speaker had known, and had endured.

"We are the Children of the Fire Mist who raised this Tower, and you who have arisen after us to dominate the worlds of this galaxy were not yet evolved from the primal slime when we ruled these stars and quit them, to venture beyond space and the limits of time itself," the ancient voice whispered.

Shastar swore under his breath, his eyes rolling with superstitious terrors, one massive hand going to his sword hilt. Ghosts out of time, speaking from the dust of dead ages! His nape-hairs prickled. But now the voice was whispering again—

"We builded this Tower as a shrine to hold our wisdom, deeply bought, and left this thought record as a testimonial to the Truth that we have learned, and which we leave as an eternal legacy to whatever race of sentient beings shall rise to inherit the galaxy after our exodus has passed . . ."

Thought record! So it was not a ghost voice from the dead past . . . and that crystal hexagon must be some sort of telepathic recording device of alien science! Thane concentrated on the faint, faint words that echoed coldly within his brain.

"You who have already attained to a technology high enough to permit your passage through Time itself, have already learned our secret and our wisdom. For the teaching we would pass on to those who come after us is legible in the unfolding history of this Universe, and you have already seen the tale unfold . . .

*and the moral of that tale should be obvious. How-
ever, I shall repeat it again."*

Illara was standing beside Thane, so close that the
warm musky scent of her hair was potent in his nostrils and vagrant tendrils of her floating hair struck
gently against the bare muscles of his shoulder like
tiny silken whips. Intently, they listened to the whispering voice.

*"You have seen life in its struggles. You have seen
empires built up with infinite toil and pain and sacrifice . . . only to fall. Bright cities have been builded
on the breast of the fair land, but be they ne'er so
bright, the breath of Time did tarnish them and they
did corrode into dust. Learn from this, then, that
material wealth and power and splendor does not
persist, and cannot be preserved against the erosion
of the ages! Learn that all the striving and strife with
which these fair cities and great empires were
builded, were wasted on a dream without substance
or permanence . . ."*

And Thane remembered again that glorious pag-
eantry of empire and conquest, as he had seen it un-
roll like rich banners of pomp and heraldry, straining
upon the black winds of time . . . and he remembered the stark ruin to which the gorgeous parade
came at the very last, and there was borne home to
him the pitiful futility of that splendor.

*"The treasure which you saw within this Tower
vanished as dust that is blown away by the first gust
of the wind. Rightly so—for all gold and treasure is
truly but bright, fragile dust! What, then, are the true
treasures to which each individual life may attain?
What goals, then, are worth striving for? What splendor is worth the strife? Only these few and humble*

things . . . the love of a mate . . . comradship of worthy friends . . . the building of a life upon the ideal of honesty and tolerance and friendship and upon respect for the rights of others. Aye! These treasures are beyond the touch of Time . . . these riches are not mere illusion . . . these things are worth fighting to acquire and to protect. Happy is he who owns such wealth; and empty and futile the life of him who has them not, aye, though a thousand stars kneel before his bright banners!"

The infinitely weary, infinitely patient voice of the Speaker whispered on, but Thane was only conscious of the warm figure of the girl standing beside him within reach of his strong arms. He turned sideway a little to look at her and saw that she was staring up at him, and that tears glimmered in the depths of her starry eyes. And suddenly the barrier that had grown up between them was breached and broken down, and both knew it was gone, and Thane knew that the only stars that he would ever own were those that glowed within her great soft eyes.

His arms were around her and the small body lay trusting against his, encircled with his mighty arms. And her small head was pillowed against his shoulder and her warm lips were seeking his hungrily, with an aching sweetness that he had never tasted on a woman's lips before . . . and great bluff Shastar was grinning at them, fiery-faced and enormously happy.

". . . Go, then, and take this simple shard of wisdom with you to your far home. For in all this Tower that we have builded up against the hand of Time, you will find no other treasure than these few words!"

And as Illara clung to him, Thane felt the beginnings of a great peace within his restless heart, and he knew that his long, long journey was ended and that he had come home at last from his far wandering. And he knew, somehow, with an inarticulate wisdom deep within his blood and bone, that he had, truly, found a treasure beyond the reach of time . . .

They passed through the portal and came outside the Tower Beyond Time and stood for a long moment staring through tears at the stark wilderness of ash and stone that lay all about the ancient and ageless structure. The sun lay on the horizon, but they could not tell whether it was sinking or rising . . . whether it signaled the end of one long day, or the beginning of a new day.

At last Shastar heaved a great gusty sigh and slapped his scabbard, looking about him.

"Well, lad . . . you have found your wench and all is well with you. And . . . what now?"

Thane smiled.

"I am not sure, chieftain! What do you suggest?"

Shastar bristled fiercely and snorted loudly in his fiery beard.

"All this talk of peace and home and fat babies . . . *pfaugh!* Not for the likes o' me—or you, either, lad. Let mumbling oldsters whisper of such in their chill senility—we have hot blood in our veins and swords ready to the hand—and, back in our own far age where we must soon return, there are worlds waiting to be won!"

"Perhaps . . ."

"Perhaps?" Shastar snorted rudely. "It's truth I speak—by Arnam's Beard and Thaxis' bloody Spear!

Nay, but, come with me, lad! Together we would make a mighty team . . . aye, I feel like a father to you, lad, for all that I, ah, once plotted and schemed against you . . . well, those times are over and done with, eh? And we have the future ahead of us, eh?"

Thane grinned and clapped the burly chieftain on the shoulder.

"Shastar, you old bandit, can you still think of crowns and conquest, after what you've heard and seen in there? You'll never change, you old rogue!"

Shastar glared and ruffled his mustachios fiercely.

"Change? I trust not, by Arnam and the Goddess Sindhi! I'm too old for change . . . but, listen, lad! You and I together, with our swords—why, we could carve out a kingdom amid the stars, you and I! Kingdom?—An *empire*—at very least! What say you, lad, eh . . . before we're too old to enjoy it?"

Thane laughed and kissed Illara till she was breathless, and turned joyous eyes on the old bandit.

"Ah . . . perhaps . . . perhaps! Who knows what may come, or what tomorrow may bring? But anyway, I know this much, you old ogre. If ever I go star-conquering or world-winning . . . I'd like to have you at my side! But first . . . first . . ."

Shastar eagerly pounced on the words as Thane's voice trailed off in a whisper.

"Aye? Aye, lad—first—*what?*"

Thane felt exaltation seethe through him like rare brandy, and he laughed boisterously, tossing back his fiery mane upon the cold thin wind. Reaching down, he scooped up the girl into his strong arms and held her tight, turning eyes that danced with mischief upon the bewildered old star pirate.

"*First* . . . I have a bit of marryin' to do!"

And, still holding her slight weight in his arms, he strode off followed by Shastar towards the Time Web and the long voyage home.

EPILOGUE

*"It was Thane who crossed the
abyss of the ages and stood on
the very brink of Eternity . . . who
found the secret of the Time Treasure
. . . who saw, and laughed, and came back
sane from that place beyond the
Universe where no man had ever been
before him, and where none should
ever come again.*

And this was the ending."

Please allow 3 weeks for filling orders.

Tower Publications, Inc., 185 Madison Ave.
New York, N.Y. 10016

Please send me the books circled above.

Amount enclosed $......... (Please add 15¢ per book for handling and postage).

ORDER BY BOOK # ONLY
CIRCLE THE NUMBER OF BOOKS WANTED

In the event we are out of stock of any of your choices, please underline the alternative *numbers*.

Name ....

(Please print.)

Address ....

City...................Zone .... State ....

Send check, cash, or money order—*NO STAMPS PLEASE.*
CANADA ONLY—add 10¢ for every Canadian dollar order. Tower Books distributed and available in British Isles at 5/– each including postage and packing from: BEN'S BOOKS COVERED MARKET, 24B Crown Street, Acton W3, London, England.